WEST RIDING COUNTY LIBRARY

This book must be returned by the last date entered above.

An extension of loan may be arranged on request if the book is not in demand.

Readers should make the fullest use of the County Library service, asking for any books and information they need.

Headquarters: Balne Lane   Telephone: 71231/4
            Wakefield

THE PLANTOS AFFAIR

By the same author

THE PLANTOS AFFAIR

by

JOHN RANKINE

London
DENNIS DOBSON

First published in Great Britain in 1971
by Dobson Books Ltd., 80 Kensington Church Street, London W.8
Printed in Great Britain by Willmer Brothers Limited, Birkenhead
Bound by C. Tinling & Co. Ltd., Prescot
ISBN 0 234 77601 3

Chapter One

At the European Space Corporation Headquarters ziggurat, in the penthouse suite, which to an outward-looking eye might have been suspended in deep space, a unilateral decision was being taken by the organization's overlord, Chairman Paul V. Spencer. He was speaking across the wide top of his executive desk to Captain Dag Fletcher and nobody would have guessed from his gravel tone that he believed the man to be the most capable commander on the company list.

Certainly his manner made no bid for empathy and the heavy, grey face was set in a hound dog mould. In fact, he was currently looking like a dog who had bitten hard on a fair bone and found that some dissembler had switched the marrow for fish paste.

'I really ought to go myself, Fletcher; but you see how it is. One blasted thing after the next on this station. If I turn my back for a nonasecond, some goddamned politician gets after the estimates and has a bonanza. Ninnyhammers all. Nothing gets done unless I slog my bowels out at this desk. So it will have to be you.'

Just in case the man should take it as a compliment, he went on, 'You are the only captain I can spare. I know you can pilot a ship. But this is something else. This needs diplomacy. You're not in the army now. If you go in as if you were part of the occupying power, you'll get nowhere fast.'

Fletcher said, 'I appreciate that, Chairman. I know the Fingalnans. They set a lot of store on keeping face. But the space corporation hook-up is in their interest as much as ours. In fact, over the decade before the agency closed, there was worthwhile payment balance in their favour. They'll agree all right. It's just a matter of moving real slow and making it appear that it was all their own idea in the first place.'

Spencer took a ruminative half minute to look at the other party in the symposium. He saw a tall, spare man, who sat relaxed, with long legs stretched out in front of him. Very brown, so that his grey-green eyes looked light by contrast. An intelligent Indo-European face, left eyebrow flared by the pull of a thin radiation burn.

There was no doubt, he was a first class commander with a legendary record as a corvette captain on his recent five-year stint with the Inter Galatic Organization's forces. If he could pull off this mission, he was that very rare bird who combined technical know-how with diplomatic skill, and was likely to be set for high office in the corporation they both served.

But it was a big question. A good measure of Spencer's disenchantment came from having to smooth out snags created by politically blinkered agents of the company and on that count, the ex-military personnel had the lousiest record.

He also had another ulcer-generating angle of personnel-management to straighten; but he approached it in a round-about way. 'All right, then, Captain. You have the mission. The company office in Fingalna has been nominally returned to our ownership; but God alone knows what state it's in. You can assess that and spend any reasonable amount to bring it up to standard. Nothing lavish, you understand, but adequate, having regard to the fact that those silvery bastards take a lot of notice of outside show. Engage local staff. Open up for business. Watch the women. As I recall, you came near to getting yourself killed by one on a recent trip.'

That was the key one, but having got it out of the way, he had another which was equally loaded.

'I'm having *Callisto* commissioned. You'll be carrying supercargo and you'll need the passenger space. I.G.O. have rounded up some top brass to re-open their consulate.'

Of the two controversial items, Dag Fletcher reckoned the last was the worst to hear. There was some justice in the

6

warning about the erotic hazards of Fingalna. They were an attractive people and natural, born intriguers. But to be given *Callisto* on a diplomatic mission was tying one hand behind his back.

He recognized that he was being given a chance to show what he could do on the admin side and that his future in the corporation hinged on making it go. There was enough there, without navigating an obsolescent tank and riding shotgun for an I.G.O. delegation.

'*Callisto?* Is that a best choice, Chairman? We want to make a good impression. She's not a modern ship.'

'I know that. But she's big. Also with the expanding service, she's the only one we have available right now without a month's wait to pull out one of the regular fleet. She's impressive. She'll look all right, I'll guarantee that. Nobody's coming aboard to check your equipment. It just means you'll have to do a little navigating instead of sitting on your ass counting stars. Here's your crew list.'

Spencer shoved a manifest slip across the desk and went on, 'All experienced. You haven't one little thing to worry about.'

Certainly, it was a solid job on paper. Some of the names Fletcher already knew. Nobody with less than two years deep space service. He had to concede that he couldn't ask for more.

Now they were names on a paper. At the end of the trip, they would be individuals, woven into the texture of his own life; so that however long or short it was, they would never be forgotten. That was one of the incidental gains of the service. There could be few other occupations where communication between people was so complete or so necessary. Otherwise no ship would make a planetfall. It was as simple as that.

The manifest read:

Ship:	*Callisto*
Mission:	Re-open Company Terminal in Fingalna
Commander:	Captain Dag Fletcher

Co-Pilot:	Captain Gary Halewood
Navigation:	1. Executive Peter Bramah
	2. Joe Ledder
	3. Executive Herbert Galloway
Power:	1. Anne Nevin
	2. Grant Rogers
	3. John Fergus
Communications:	1. Executive Trudy Brogan
	2. Fred Mercer
	3. Alex McGee
Factor:	Sub Controller A. J. Crowhurst
Assistants:	Milton Hine
	Lorna Miment
On Passage:	I.G.O. Commissar Sarpedon
	Assistant Commissar Entema
	Assistant Commissar Hulda

Fletcher said, 'I'll take the mission, Chairman. But I want it made clear from the start that this I.G.O. detachment are passengers only. No privileged status.'

'That's okay. I'll see they understand. Actually they're in our debt. There isn't a regular flight they can take for another two months. And that's a slow freighter. They'll behave. Observers pure and simple.'

To any observer couched on cosmic dust and indulging a taste for philosophy, the wandering, artificial asteroid that housed the machinery for galactic entente was a potent symbol of the spirit of co-operation. It was incredible that it should have been built, a continuing miracle that it survived to exercise a peace-keeping role over distances that made Alexander's empire an exercise in a play pen.

Maybe a built-in survival instinct had prompted the founding planets not to sell short and to send able administrators on secondment. Certainly a long line of chief officials in the hot seat as President of the Regulating Council of the Inter Galactic Organization had kept the balance of power with infinite skill and built up an enduring authority.

En-Liarri, the nineteenth president, a grey-skinned hexapod from Centaurus was no exception. It had fallen on him to weather the storm of the recent challenge made by a consortium of the militant planets of the Rim. His decision had brought together the most powerful force in the violent history of man to disperse the insurgent fleets of the Outer Galactic Alliance in one definitive stroke.

With a year of office still to run he aimed to hand over to his successor a galaxy at peace.

On the face of it, that was a reasonable ambition. After the upheaval, the insurgents had gone quiet and seemed to have accepted the situation; even to the extent of allowing I.G.O. consulates in their capital cities where none had been before; even to a nominal declaration that they would accept the I.G.O. Charter of Human Rights.

But the very completeness of success spelled danger to a subtle mind. Forces that had precipitated the bid for power were not likely to disperse in a mist of goodwill. En-Liarri had given it a lot of thought. He was convinced that the O.G.A. hard core planets had not suffered a revolutionary change of heart. Certainly Scotia would not change with its feudal, military economy and its population of subhuman, reptilian hatchet men. Or Chrysaor, the golden planet, with its acute population pressures and traditional aim to expand by conquest.

In the inner council of six, he voiced his misgivings, speaking in a slow, quiet voice into the multivox which worked a quick shuffle and channelled it out six ways in six different tongues.

At the receiving end of the English version, Commissar Ledsham, the delegate from Earth planet, thought he was hearing the understatement of all time. Relatively new to the council, after a long stint on diplomatic service in a half dozen capitals on the frontiers of the Rim powers, he knew

A*

for a truth that only expedient caution would be holding Scotia back. They would be biding their time. The lesson they had learned was not that war does not pay; but that losing this particular war proved that they had not prepared for it well enough.

It was also true that a large number of uncommitted planetary governments, who had remained neutral in the I.G.O.—O.G.A. confrontation, were rushing to pick up trade links with the ringleaders as though nothing out-of-the-way had occurred.

Maybe that was not too significant. A quick dollar had its lustre wherever it was picked up. But they were the ones who would have jumped gladly on the band-waggon of an O.G.A. success. The terms of the I.G.O. charter bore heavily on certain anti-social practices that went on within their own borders.

En-Liarri listened to six statements, all calling for caution. They confirmed his own reading of the score. It was a saddening gloss on the years of patient building. There was no final security. He was reminded of the dictum that in a long confrontation with a high-level civilization, the forces of barbarism were the ones that won out. A little folding of the hands, a little sleep and the great, peaceful cultures of the Galaxy could be swept away.

Eternal vigilance was the price that had to be paid for the privilege of sleeping safe in a bed.

Commissar Labasha of Kuros brought up a new point. Using basic speech tones, the lingua franca of the Galaxy, he reminded the council of the informed rumour that detailed treaty commitments had been settled between O.G.A. and the neutrals. If such a document indeed existed, it would be a potent help in sorting friend from foe and would give I.G.O. intelligence a flying start in knowing where to look for any new build-up of power.

En-Liarri was unexpectedly irritable. Only a bland form of words filtered through the multivox, but his face was there to mirror it. 'That is all very well. Such a document may well have existed and it would be of great value; but we cannot suppose that it has not been destroyed by all parties or that any copy of it could be taken without a war of attrition on one of the O.G.A. capitals.'

Ledsham said, 'Intelligence reports at the time said that the flagship *Leviathon* made the diplomatic round to get signatures. It could be that a copy was retained on that ship by the high command of the O.G.A. forces.'

Labasha said, 'That is more than likely. Do we have any knowledge of the present location of that ship?'

En-Liarri keyed the question into his console and switched the response direct to the multivox. They heard, '*Leviathon*. Fingalnan super ship. Commissioned 2261. Last commanded by Admiral Xantu. Used in C-in-C of O.G.A. combined operations force. Escaped general destruction of O.G.A. fleets and was hunted for two years by an I.G.O. squadron under Admiral Varley. Finally run to earth on Plantos-Three and disabled by fragmentation charges. Crew, including Admiral Xantu, brought back for war crimes trial. All prohibited from future military service and restricted to home planets on a probationary basis reporting to I.G.O. correspondents every three months.'

Ledsham said, 'Disabled is not destroyed. Such a document would not be kept with the usual ship's papers. If it existed it could still be there.'

The delegate from Kronos, Abisare, put in, 'A super ship is not a coracle. Finding it would not be easy. Also to send a military ship to the dead world of Plantos would advertise what we were doing. Concealment would not be possible. I agree that it would be useful to have; but there are so many imponderables, it could be wiser to let it lie there.'

There was a five second pause before En-Liarri delivered a judgement. 'I believe we should make the attempt. I will speak to the Chairman of the Enforcement Division, he might have some suggestions. Also Admiral Varley. He is still in service with the patrol fleet. It is an avenue which must be checked out.'

A commander new to the commissioning chore might justifiably have reckoned that he had been given a draft of psychotics from a therapy centre. But Dag Fletcher knew that he would see a different side when they were out of Earth's gravisphere. Also, from long use, he suspended judgement. First impressions were almost always wrong. The longer you could delay putting a label on a man, the more likely you were to find the right one.

On paper, it had been a neat and tidy operation. On the ground, there appeared to be many more than fourteen human primates milling about inside *Callisto*. And as yet the three diplomats had not appeared to add their mite of stress.

Suspension of judgement was a necessary technique. Fighting for sectional priorities, the three executives kept up a running fire of demand.

Herb Galloway, a small, energetic Scot had come fresh from a mission in one of the latest fleet numbers. He was at first incredulous and then bitterly sarcastic about the ageing power pack he was expected to superintend. His final request for a total replacement of the port booster was in the form of an ultimatum, delivered with a kettle-drum roll of intrusive r's, 'There's a bare eighty per cent efficiency, Commander, and that's the truth. I tell you, I'll not be responsible. It's every man and woman on board that's at risk.'

Knocking off a margin for a perfectionist, Fletcher reckoned they would get by on a straightforward, planet-to-planet hop.

More difficult to deal with was Trudy Brogan. As one of the few women executives in the service, she had to be that much tougher to make it clear that sex was no handicap. Small and trim, with a hood of shining black hair and a face that could have been chipped off an Egyptian mural, she appeared in the hatch of the factor's office which was the nerve centre of the commissioning exercise.

12

A natural warm-brown contralto had to work at it to be icy; but there was no mistaking the tone when she said, 'I would be glad of a minute of your time, Commander.'

Dressed in a black, one-piece coverall with a round, stand-up collar and the corporation insignia presented on the pleasing curve of the left breast pocket, she was entitled to claim more.

Fletcher had the knack of making everyone feel that he had all the time in the world for their problem. He said, 'What is it, executive?'

Some of the arctic chill went out of her voice but it was still less than cordial. 'You are aware that, in the middle passage, we shall be out of range of this control for a two-way link?'

'I know it. That's the way it was for the first century of space travel. What's so bad? You can talk to me. Anything we might want to say out there only has academic interest for base. Freighters still operate that way. I reckon it will be for under twenty-four hours, rationalized time.'

She looked surprised, 'So you know?'

'That's so. Look, if it was a difficult mission, I'd insist on a refit. As it is, there's no problem. We have a time line to beat. You'll be shopping around in Argentus for pleasing, feminine trifles before you've warmed your executive seat.'

Callisto might well be a goodly apple rotten at the heart; but to the outward eye, Spencer had done an impressive job. She was refurbished in vermilion-lustre with ports and hatches picked out in black and the blue-and-white Earth blazon on a two-metre square panel below the cone. She dwarfed the more modern ships in the port. At Argentus, the Fingalnan capital, she would be the most eye-catching artifact on the set.

Incredibly, the work was done. Three hours before blast-off, Fletcher revolved slowly on the command island in *Callisto's* control cabin and ran the penultimate check.

He was well-satisfied. In Gary Halewood he had a Number One who was as meticulous as himself in setting standards,

13

with the additional virtue that he really enjoyed being particular and caring for detail. Fletcher liked order; but he knew that on a long haul he was likely to run out on consistent attention to the small print. It was important to have a running mate who would cover that angle.

Maybe there would be no earth-shattering original thought from Halewood, but in the last analysis he would be found with a full due of equipment all in top-level trim.

Also, reviewing the manifest, Fletcher was pleased to report to himself that he was going to have no personal sex problem rearing its seductive head. Trudy Brogan, in spite of appearances had a fixation for her computers. Anne Nevin, a plump blonde who could have modelled for a Renoir *baigneuse,* only had eyes for the executive of her section and Bramah, the navigation number one, a thin sad-faced type, took no notice; because he, in turn, was doing his best in competition with the hardware to interest Trudy Brogan. A nicely sealed circle of involvement with no valencies free.

Lorna Diment, assistant to the factor was a natural comedian and underlined the view that laughter routs Eros. Averagely good-looking with a long-legged athletic figure, she was accepted as a non-erotic object. In the wardroom, she was mainly to be found, thumbs in a narrow snakeskin belt, leaning on the bar and swapping unlikely commercial stories with her fellow entrepreneur Milton Hine for the edification of John Fergus the power number three.

Two hours from zero, Fletcher called the penthouse.

Spencer's large grey face filled the scanner like a kilogram of putty, 'What is it?'

'All set, Chairman. I thought you would like a personal report. No sign yet of the diplomatic party, but their gear is aboard.'

'They'll be along.'

'Could I ask, when?'

'You know these people, Fletcher. If we ran a space line in the same last-minute panic that they run their affairs, we'd be out of business. Reckon on thirty minutes before lift-off.'

'That's neat. There's a whole raft of weight ratios to work as soon as they're in place. That's my outside limit. After 1630, they don't get a ride.'

'You say.'

'I say. 1700 on the nose gives us the best vectors for a fortnight. We want all the advantages we can get from nature her own self.'

'I'll talk to them. Meanwhile, good luck.'

'Thank you. You can tell them 1631 will be too late. The seals will be on.'

At 1625, Halewood was looking anxious. 'I heard what you said to Spencer, Dag. But I wouldn't advise it. That one has a long memory.'

'I'll answer for it. We need an optimum conjunct.'

He went through the preliminary drills and called John Fergus in his emergency control centre above the radiation bulkhead to close hatches.

The tally showed on a schematic diagram of *Callisto* in a panel of the main scanner. Red tell-tales blinked to green as the seals went on in progression from the lowest freight bay, until there was only one left, below the company blazon at the highest level of the gantry.

Halewood said, 'Hold fast at that, Power Three.'

A black-and-red shuttle with an I.G.O. pennant streaming stiffly back was coming urgently from the headquarter complex. It disappeared behind the blockhouse and with half a minute to Fletcher's dead line, an elevator cage began its run up the tower.

Incoming personnel would now have a ten-metre walk along a high, narrow catwalk. Fletcher, watching grimly from the panoramic, direct-vision port, set at the tape in the waist, thought it might serve as a spur to time-keeping. He had a foreshortened view of three figures crossing the ramp. Even at the distance, it was clear that two were male and the rear-guard was female and nubile at that.

15

He had a sudden mental picture of the view from the gangplank with its uninterrupted drop of two hundred metres to the parquet, then they were inside and as her back disappeared into the hatch, Halewood's voice on the intercom said, 'All right, Power Three, wrap it up.'

He was left with a niggling sense of disquiet. There was something about the way she walked that spelled out a certain kind of elegance that he had always found disturbing to his peace of mind. Another adjustment to make, before he could claim to be flame-proof from the erotic hazards of the voyage.

Galloway came up with a piece of grief wrapped in official-ese that did nothing to make it less.

'Power one to Commander.'

'Go ahead.'

'Two hundred kilos on the diplomatic hoof. Distributed 78, 70, 52. I had provisional estimates for 175. This reduces margins. Still viable, but getting delicate and that's the truth.'

'Thank you. I'll watch it.'

Two hundred kilos of biological tissue up top would make the ship very tender. Also his power-to-weight ratio was being steadily eroded. The 52 element would be the girl.

He found himself saying to Halewood, 'Carry on. I'll go and welcome the supercargo. See that they settle in straight away.'

At the back of his mind, he knew that primate curiosity was pushing it along. He wanted to see, first hand, how the 52 kilo package was organized.

One thing was for sure, when he reached the passenger cabin. He was not dealing with amateurs. The three diplomats had already broken out space gear from the racks and were angling the acceleration couches on their universal bearings to give an optimum balance of weight through 360 degrees.

Curiosity, evolution's midwife, met a check. She was anonymous in a bulky, steel-grey suit; but the visor, hinged back, was making a frame for a head that justified the journey on its own account.

16

A name tag with the I.G.O. motif of a black, equilateral spiral on a red ground, top left and the four moons of Bromius, top right, said, *Hulda*.

So she was a Bromusian by origin. Some admixture of race, through, in the ancestral tree. Pure stock of that refined culture ran to dark hair and pale-coffee skin. Hulda was fair. Hair like an electrum bell, magnolia skin, eyes large, wide and flecked grey. Generous mouth, opened in that diplomatic smile of welcome which the naked ape of every planet used to disarm aggression.

Fletcher said curtly, 'Glad to have you aboard *Callisto*. Lift off at 1700 as you know. I'll signal when you can leave the couches. Probably one hour from now, unless we meet any snags. Do you have any questions?'

The girl continued to smile and he had an uneasy feeling that she knew exactly why he had made the trip. Belatedly, he remembered that E.S.P. was an advanced science on Bromius. Very likely, any lecherous thought would be picked up before he had identified it himself. Confirmation came as the smile switched off and the eyes continued to look amused.

Answer, when it came, was from the senior partner, labelled *Sarpedon: I.G.O. Commissar* and clearly the proud owner of the 78 kilos. It was delivered by a gutteral voice using the speech-tone system. Symbol identification put him as a Mensanite from one of the small planets on the Rim. Another group which had been technically advanced when Earth primates had still been debating whether it was an okay thing to come down out of the trees.

'That is quite clear, Commander. You will find us co-opera-tive. We are, in a manner of speaking, on the same kind of mission.'

At the same time, he fixed Fletcher with a bright stare from triangularly hooded eyes as though he was weighing him in a private balance for some special project of his own devising.

Dag Fletcher was nettled by it. Already aware that he should have made his greeting over the tannoy, he resented

17

being patronized on his own ship, as though these two felt themselves better qualified by intellect to make any decisions that were called for, and were letting him pilot the boat as a courtesy gesture.

Number three of the trio was less outgoing. He was already prudently sealed up and was buckling himself on to his couch. Bright, nervous eyes, black as polished obsidian peered up at the Earthman. His suit was tagged, *Entema* with the blazon of Kuros.

Back at his console, Fletcher cleared his mind of every other issue and prepared for lift-off.

There was a last minute message from Spencer, before the video line was dropped. The verbal side was scrambled on the company's code and the screen remained blank with only the corporation insignia to show the office of origin. He went into it without preamble. 'Something on the grapevine from Western Hemisphere. *Through* Western Hem, I should judge; because the point of origin may be higher up. A government department is looking around for a private charter out in your area. Could be the first piece of business for the new office. If it comes our way, cost it low. I'll hold the next freighter until I hear from you. Not a word about it, mind, until you're approached, I get my information by a very devious channel.'

It was another matter to file in the back of his mind, meanwhile there was the business of accepting crew reports from Halewood, although he had already listened on the general net to the exchanges between the executives and the co-pilot.

Bramah's voice, clipped and precise as a maiden aunt, 'Navigation. All Systems Go.'

Galloway leaning heavily on the only uvular consonant he could find, 'Power. All Systems Go.'

Trudy Brogan making a viola entry of it, 'Communications. All Systems Go.'

Halewood said formally, 'Number One to Commander.

All Systems Go,' and made it official.

Fletcher said briefly, 'Check,' and shoved home the link which allowed automation to plod on into the final stage. Ten seconds now with a sweep hand knocking them off. Nothing to do but wait and not a thing any power on earth could do to stop *Callisto*.

Even after the years of experience it was always new. A rebirth into another dimension, where anything was possible. He felt a rising tide of nervous tension tighten his throat. They were the living dead, waiting for revelation. Still bound to Earth; but no longer any part of it. Who was to say that *Callisto's* power pack would deliver under control. One of these days, he would be detonating a bomb when he shoved over that lever.

Then she was moving and the gantry was falling away. The impossible was happening over again. In the stern sector of the multiscreen, he could see the dwindling circle of the space port cut by an arc of incandescent, orange flame, where the fireball was nudging into the field of vision.

At the same time, he became aware that he was also seeing it from the contrary angle, so that the picture was plastic, in soft focus. The orange bite was swinging to the opposite diameter and back again.

For a second's panic, Fletcher thought the rigorous physical check, taken as standard requirement for the mission, had not been searching enough. As yet, there was no G to speak of. If he was on the blink already, he should sign himself off and leave it to Halewood.

Part of the fluctuating picture showed the cowling of the port rocket nacelle. That was more than double vision. How could he be seeing that?

Schematic diagrams of the ship's communication system flipped through his mind's eye. Surely, that was the view they would be getting on the scanner in the passenger cabin?

It was Hulda. Probably nervous at take off and doing a little indiscriminate mental broadcasting, which he was picking up. Must be on her natural wavelength. It was a long coincidence; but if it was so she could exploit the situation anytime she liked.

'Number One. Any fluctuation in multiscreen scans?'

'Not a thing. Rock steady all round the ship.'

'Check.'

He concentrated on projecting an outgoing, confident set, a psychokinetic morale-building job. Maybe it was his own introspective uncertainty that had triggered off her apprehension and given it a toe-hold.

That figured. Who more likely for a nervous passenger to contact than the captain? He thought it through in words, making it clear that there was no problem, that they were in a well-found ship with every prognosis of a successful voyage.

The screen cleared. She had gotten herself sorted. It was, however, one more imponderable. Whenever he was near her, he would have to make sure that he kept anything on the restricted list out of the transfer areas of his mind.

With *Callisto* out of Earth's gravisphere, warped into rationalized time and buttoned down on minimum watch details, he had the leisure to work on the theory.

He came up behind her in the wardroom as she stood at the dispenser making an aesthete's choice of dietary items. Out of her shell, it was a recognizable fact that every one of the fifty-two kilos did a positive job to give any reasonable observer food for vision, and much brooding thought was as out of place as a nun at a coven. Long supple legs, delicate arms and shoulders, metallic hair caught smoothly back in an amber filigree clasp—bromide would be a better national adjective than Bromusian.

Callisto's wardroom was big enough to leave a gap between them and the group already sitting at the long centre table. Lorna Diment, anyway, was putting out enough grooming noise to act as a sonic screen and they were for the moment, isolated in a small intimate enclave.

She turned suddenly to face him and said, 'But bromides

are for sleep, Commander. I can promise you, I am very wide awake.'

It was proof enough. Fletcher said, 'Who could doubt it? I had in mind the outgoing effect.'

'Flattery will get you nowhere.'

'I had no particular place in view. But flattery suggests deception. There is no deception. Doesn't it take all the pleasure out of the social exchange to know ahead what people think?'

'Some of the pleasure. Almost all the disappointment. But in fact, I don't always know. It's just that you are particularly easy for me to read.'

'Thank you very much. Just a simple savage.'

Hulda considered him squarely, flecked eyes very candid. 'Not so. You are far from simple. It is an accident. Your mental rhythms happen to coincide with a harmonic of my own. I showed you this to warn you that it was so. I shall not pry. Indeed it is not possible unless you allow it.'

Callisto reeled back the meaningless distances, a bobbin on the fine thread spun by her computers. The crew became a team. Fletcher reckoned it was the least eventful passage he had made in any ship. As far as he could judge, Hulda was as good as her word.

When Fingalna was plate-size on the main scanner he warped out of rationalized time, hitting schedules to the precise second. As they entered the gravisphere of the silver planet, Trudy Brogan came up, pat on cue, 'Four to Commander. Argentus control calling on direct speech. Request clearance.'

'Go ahead.'

It was too easy. There was a brief flash from Hulda as he turned the ship to bring them down. It was a confused picture, which cleared quickly as retro fired and *Callisto* slowed for the pad. Obviously, when emotion moved her, she transmitted like a beacon.

Then *Callisto* was flexing majestically on her hydraulic jacks and a cloud of grey coolant was damping out the thermal jig.

As the mist thinned from direct vision ports, the neighbouring ship stopped wavering and showed up in clear definition, even to the name *Agron* in gothic script at her wasp waist.

Dag Fletcher stared in open disbelief. The last time he had seen her twin was from the command island of a hard-pressed corvette with every expectation that the next nonasecond would be his last. She was a Scotian. Dwarfed on the ground by *Callisto's* towering bulk, but infinitely deadly. A slim, black-and-yellow pointer of destruction.

If he had made the planetfall in a military ship, his first act would have been to swing the main armament to bear as a routine safeguard. As it was, there was only the frail screen of diplomatic usage to rely on and he knew for a truth that it would only serve for as long as it suited *Agron's* Commander.

Hulda had picked up his concern and he felt her query; but it faded quickly as he broadcast a non-verbal equivalent to, 'Mind your own damned business.'

Aloud, he said, 'Communications. Get me Argentus control. I want to know why they've brought us in next to this pot of poison.'

Chapter Two

From the pad, Argentus appeared to be unchanged. Ringed by bare, silvery hills, it was one of the showplaces of the galaxy, a considerable ornament of time.

Population knocking the maximum of four million and the site restricted to an elliptical plain, it had opted for vertical growth. Walkways and escalator ramps, like delicate flying buttresses, festooned the set—shining streamers over a fantastic Emmet-land.

At the northern end of the long, north-south axis of the site, the space port was virtually isolated from the city. Terminal buildings ran in a solid dyke, east-west, and dovetailed into living rock. On the perimeter, slopes had been cut back to an arc of sheer cliff. There was only one way out and that was through the filter of the official exit.

To get permission to use *Callisto's* tender instead of a hire car with a Fingalnan driver, took a day of patient negotiation.

Finally, Fletcher set out to check the corporation's remaining real estate, with Fergus in the pilot seat and Crowhurst and Lorna Diment as business consultants in the rumble.

There was one Scotian in the circular entrance hall, well-placed to watch for any movement of personnel. A lean satanshape. Bluish-white skin, hairless head, long El-Greco distortion of the universal hominoid physique. He was armed with a heavy-calibre laser, which seemed incongruous in the prevailing anti-military climate. An olive-drab uniform fitted like an integral skin. Cold-blooded and insensitive to opinion, he would stay there like a maypole, if the lobby were to fill with a maenad rout of nude Bacchantes.

His eyes licked coldly over the group and came back to

Lorna Diment. She got the message, even over a gap of seventy-five metres, and shivered involuntarily.

Fergus, walking beside her, put in a totally unhelpful gloss. 'Somebody walking over your grave?'

'I've got a feeling that one would dig it up like a regular ghoul.'

'He might at that. They're not fastidious. A taut, dark number in crimson pants would switch him full on.'

There was a wait of ten minutes for the car to appear from the freight subway. Then a hectic thirty minutes with Fergus taking time to adjust to the febrile confusion of city traffic, before they homed on a parking lot in Government Square.

The company office was on the forty-first floor of a tower block, flanked by administrative buildings and carrying on its porch the optimistic legend, 'Galactic Harmony House.' An indicator board in the lobby read like a nominal roll of the chief trading planets of the galaxy.

European Space Corporation Earth Planet, shared a line with a mining company from Sabazius, whose strip looked pristine fresh like a new addition to the club. A reception kiosk with stations for five clerks had only one grille open for trade and a clerical android watched them cross the parquet without stopping a busy typing ploy on its desk console.

Fletcher used speech tones and it managed to sound surprised.

'Is the office suite on forty-one ready for occupation?'

'Ready for occupation?'

'I have clearance from the Trade Council. I'm re-opening the European Space Terminal.'

'European Space Terminal?'

Lorna Diment said, 'It's little Sir Echo in person. What's his problem?'

She spoke in English and the robot picked up the problem bit and lifted a prehensile grab to twist a speech change knob,

24

which it carried in lieu of a left ear. Then it answered in
the same tongue. 'Yes, there is a problem. The rooms are not
ready.'

'Can we see them?'

'It is not convenient.'

'Who says it is not convenient?'

It was a key question and the android was saved embarras-
ment by the bell. A tell-tale blinked on his console and an
elevator homed on its pad in the facing wall. Four passengers
were decanted by the moving footplate and made a bee line
for the porch. Three were Fingalnans dwarfed by the fourth,
who was a Scotian in civilian rig, which was nothing more
than a uniform without rank flashes.

Fletcher said, 'Don't give it another thought.' He stretched
a long arm over the counter, picked a serrated number disk
off a long filing panel on the reredos and led the way to
the empty cage.

As the elevator began to move, he saw the android stub a
button on his call board.

Fergus said, 'What was all that about, Commander?'

'You tell me.'

It was clearer when they saw the office.

The disk, dropped in a slot, activated a motor and lifted a
bronze grille that masked the regular door. The inside leaves
slid away at a touch into the thickness of the wall. Inside,
there was room to get in and take a look; but after saying
that, there was no more on the credit side. It was packed from
floor to ceiling with a junkyard collection of lumber that must
have been collected from every office in the building.

Lorna Diment ran a supple finger over a specimen. 'You
know, I wouldn't say this has been here very long. Not *years*
anyway. There's no dust on it.'

Fletcher thought, 'That figures. Probably organized by the
Scotian as a delaying tactic. Though hardly worth the effort.
It can be cleared up in a couple of days.'

Aloud, he said to Crowhurst, 'I'll call the Trade Council

and get it shifted. Meanwhile have a look round and get some ideas for the refit. John, you nip downstairs and get a list of addresses from the mechanical wonder. Names of local staff who ever worked for European Space. We can't do anything without personnel, so maybe it's just as well to cover that angle first. I'll go next door and wave the flag at the mining camp.'

Waiting on the mat for welcome to come up in lights, Dag Fletcher considered the Sabazius interest. A small, backward planet in the neutral belt between I.G.O. and O.G.A. space, unless there had been revolutionary changes, it was not in the race for industrial empire building.

The door slid back. It was a suite similar to their own. A hundred square metres of floor space in the main room and four ante-chambers opening off. Colour schemes in heavy blues and purples went some way to defeat the Fingalnan daylight and present a subterranean image.

Three Sabazians, two male and one opulently female, stopped their toil at the coal face and watched him in. A typical rep of the ethnic stock, heaved himself over to the counter and stood waiting to hear what it was all about.

At just under two metres, Fletcher was tall by Earth standards; but the Sabazian was looking down at him. Bulky and barrel-chested, with a round grey head, his eyes, many-faceted and black as polished obsidian, gave nothing away. The nudge of a sixth sense signalled to Fletcher that they knew all about him and that in some sense his visit was expected.

He went for a formal opening, knowing that the Sabazians had a Prussian attitude to protocol. 'Commander Fletcher, European Space Corporation, I'd be glad of your co-operation about staff.'

'In what way?'

'You will have experience about recruitment. What agency did you use?'

'We are not a general trading company. We do not need to employ local staff.'

There was a gutteral comment from one of the supporter's club and the other one leaned back in her chair to give free passage for an unexpectedly high-pitched, sycophant's giggle, which set up a vibration under her smock like a shock wave in jelly.

The front man showed his appreciation by writhing back his lips in a soundless laugh that mimed contempt in any language.

Dag Fletcher took a count of five to consider it. Diplomacy was fine up to a point; but this type had to be clubbed over the head at regular intervals before they appreciated the vocabulary. At the same time, he was aware that a third force had gotten in on the act. Before his very eyes, the Sabazian office was overlaid by a wavering double image seen from an opposite viewpoint, as though he was, simultaneously, behind and in front of the reception desk.

The secondary scene was a busy lobby and he recognized the shadowy bulk of Sarpedon just on the periphery of vision. So it was Hulda again. Somewhere near. Very likely in a neighbouring block.

For a split second, he felt his mind reinforced as though they had hit a common frequency and he was seeing past the obsidian barrier of the Sabazian's eyes to a knowledge of what lay behind. The man knew all about the city dump in the European Space office and had in fact been part of the organizing force.

The delay was taken by the Sabazian for indecision, springing from weakness. He put both hands on the counter and leaned forward to push the message across. 'The door is behind you, Earthman.'

Fletcher came back to the here and now and moved with deceptive, casual speed. Knocking simultaneously left and right with flat hands, he shifted the biped supports, so that gravity worked to bring the man's head down. Then he helped it along with a double grip on the back of his neck and brought it with a meaty thud to meet the desk top.

The humorist grabbed for a desk drawer and the giggler was suddenly still, caught by surprise like a leaned-back Henry Moore monumental figure.

Fletcher spoke from the door. 'If that's the way you want it, that's the way it is.'

John Fergus followed him in to the home pad. 'No joy, Commander. The tin gnome reckons they're all dispersed. In work they won't want to change. I have one name; but he's over working age. Used to be chief clerk here. Ur-Ilbaba. He wound up the business when the Europeans pulled out. He's located in the twenty-ninth precinct. House ref. 53/0/10-16.'

Crowhurst said, 'That's a down town area, and a zero ref puts him in a basement. Ten levels below ground in fact. He didn't do too well out of company service.'

From the window, Lorna Diment said, 'But he would know about what happened to the others.' Her voice quickened as she went on. 'There's a security car coming this way across the square.'

Once again, Fletcher had a racing flash of insight. The car was responding to the android's call. There was no serious charge that could be made, but once inside a precinct guard house, there could be all kinds of delay.

They were out of the elevator and halfway across the lobby when the gendarmerie appeared from the street. Fletcher went directly to one marked out by elaborate epaulettes as a top hand. He said, 'Commander Fletcher, European Space. I am glad to know that you answer calls so fast. There has been an accident on floor forty-one—the mining company. Nothing serious, but I guess our tin man here likes to be sure.'

The section-leader looked past him to the android, who was waiting to be asked a civil question. A human operator would have been round the desk, putting in the boot; but mechanization knew its place. Surface courtesy won out. He said, 'Very well, Commander. I will look into it.'

Working the traffic flow from first principles, Fergus took the nearest radial lane to make out for a concentric to the suburbs. Seen close, the city had small accretions of decay which escalated into areas of seedy dilapidation in the twenty-ninth precinct. Here, street signs were first casualties in the prevailing rot and, all-in-all, it was a full hour before they had picked out block fifty-three. A small snowstorm of trash rose round the car as Fergus dropped them on its unswept porch.

At the janitor's desk, a small wrinkled woman, who was not pure-stock Fingalnan, grappled with speech tones as though they were a tricky code. 'Ur-Ilbaba? There are so many tenants, how could I remember all the names? But zero-ten, that is downwards.' She pointed to the floor with a withered claw. 'Perhaps the other strangers looked for him also. Two sets of strangers in one day. That is unusual.'

'Others?'

'About twenty minutes ago. Two men. Very tall. Very ugly.' Claw hands drew a cartoon of bloated bulk in the dusty air. 'They did not speak to me, but they went below. That way.'

Trogs of block fifty-three had no benefit of elevator service. A system of stairs and ramps led down from the lobby. Ceiling ports every five metres injected a measured ration of daylight simulate, but after the sixth level, there were long gaps with many no longer lit.

On a busy day, it would be difficult to avoid knocking into people travelling for the surface. As it was, the occasional commuter hurried by, close to the right-hand wall, where the surface was worn smooth by many trailing hands.

At level ten, they had adjusted to a grey twilight. Underfoot, they were walking on a thick carpet of trash with a heavy scent of antiseptics drugging the breath.

Crowhurst said, 'I reckon they find it cheaper to spray round with a bug killer than muck out the garbage. There's a triumph for medical science.'

Larger, resistant strains had come through unscathed, however. Lorna Diment, who had gotten herself ahead, wanting to see the chore wound up, let out an 'Eek' that made a period and fairly threw herself at Fergus.

A dark stain undulated out of the line of march with dry, scrabbling noises.

She said, 'It was *soft*. I touched it with my *toes*.'

'Walk boldly in my footsteps like that page.'

Twenty metres on, Fletcher stopped suddenly in a dark section and the column telescoped behind him. The squaw blundered into Fergus's back with a jar that rattled her teeth.

Fletcher said, 'Apartment sixteen.'

Other doors on the level had been ajar and gave signs of a better light source inside. This one swung open at a touch, but led into deeper darkness.

Fergus fished a pencil torch out of his breast pocket and shone it around, earning himself a rebuke.

'You selfish *swine*, John. Why didn't you bring that out before. Then I wouldn't have walked on that creature.'

'Just a device to bring out the clinging side of your nature.'

Crowhurst located a switch and a ceiling port glowed with light. There was not a lot to see. Ur-Ilbaba had cut down on consumer items. There was a chair, a table and a wall bed partly retracted in its alcove. The floor was swept clean. On the wall, beside the bed, was a familiar blazon, a blue and white representation of Earth planet with a garland of olive leaves and the pocket motif of European Space.

Fletcher said slowly, 'He's hung on to that through some very dodgy times. I'd guess he was a loyal employee of the company and the connection has not helped him. Whether he can still work or not, we'll have him out of here and put him back on the payroll.'

A born fiddler, Lorna Diment pressed the release button and the bed dropped out for inspection.

Now it was clear why it had not homed snugly in its niche. Ur-Ilbaba was still in it.

He was, however, beyond the reach of question and answer. A loop of metal cloth had been passed round his neck and twisted tourniquet-wise by a half metre of tubular rod broken from the bedframe. His tongue had forced itself out between his teeth and his eyes were fixed in protuberant agony. One arm was strained back like a pointer behind his head and its fingers were sticky with the silvery ichor which was the Fingalnan permutation of life's blood.

It was a fair confirmation that ill-fortune went in a run of three and one farther on than stubbing a bare toe on a rodent. The proposition that primate curiosity worked on the side of evolution, took a knock. Too shocked for an 'Eek', she stood still as any stone.

Fergus turned her away and had to force her to sit in the chair.

Fletcher said bitterly, 'Within the hour. We signed his warrant as soon as we asked for his number.'

'Who would know,'—Crowhurst had not made the addition—'There was only the android at the desk. We didn't advertise it.'

Fergus left his zombie, 'We were in the office when I told you the address.'

Belatedly, Dag Fletcher remembered that the Sabazians had expected his call. They had been given all the time in the world to set up a listening post in the neighbour office. But it was hardly a Sabazian angle. They might not welcome Earth personnel; but there was no direct, trade rivalry. They were only agents in the exercise, passing information to a more active O.G.A. partner. Which in this instance was likely to be the Scotian.

Confirmation came as Crowhurst said, 'He was still alive when they tipped him in there. See the marks on the panel.'

'More than that,' Fletcher lifted the small body clear to look down into the recess. 'He was trying to put the finger on his executioner.'

Twisted over and using Fergus's torch to beat the shadow, he saw that the scribble was more than a random act. In his last brief ration of time, Ur-Ilbaba had kept enough control to saw open his skin on a rough edge and use a finger as a flow pen. The diamond moment of death had come in mid composition; but there was no doubt that he was using phonetic symbols for speech tone and that he had gotten as far as a shaky version of SCOT.

Fletcher heaved himself out of the hole. Ur-Ilbaba was a person of no importance, an ex-servant of the company, unemployable maybe, eking out his days in a squalid cellar; but he was what organized government was all about. In the last analysis, there had to be an authority backed with force that guaranteed the right of the meek to keep their tithe of Earth after they had inherited it.

In many a long haul on a military mission, Fletcher had found himself questioning the moral sanction that lay behind what he was doing. It had always ended as an open question, with the demands of action short-circuiting the argument and the over-riding drive for survival coming top of the heap.

Now, as a civilian, without the backing of mega-power under his thumb, he could appreciate the bitter frustration of the victimized man.

When the Scotian had come through the door, there was nothing the old Fingalnan could do except endure. Nowhere to turn for justice. The most agonized prayer he could make would not stir a blade of grass. Now, he himself was powerless to make whatever redress was possible to a corpse.

The least he could do, however, was put him back on his bed. Crowhurst had the same idea, and although the weight was hardly a burden for two, there was some psychological comfort in sharing the guilt of disturbing the body again. The enterprise was in train, with Lorna Diment watching wide-eyed, as though she had unexpectedly come across a Burke and Hare documentary sequence, when the room appeared to fill with security details.

A number count showed that there were only five. Two had crossed to the far wall and covered the set with riot-blasters. The leader of the force, wearing the rank flashes of a sub-controller of police, had every reason to expect co-operation, when he said, 'So our information was correct, the Earthmen are trouble-makers. You will come to precinct headquarters.'

Fletcher said, 'Hold it there. Are you thinking we killed this man?'

'Thinking? I have the evidence of my eyes. See, he is still bleeding.'

'Before we move, I want a representative of the I.G.O. consulate brought here.'

'That is not necessary. You will be allowed to contact a legal office. We are not primitives.'

'Who will record the time of our arrival here and the time of this man's death? He was already dead when we arrived. The janitor said that other visitors had enquired for this level.'

'There is no janitor at the desk. Where is she now?'

Lorna Diment broke a long, Trappist silence, 'But there was an old woman. Dark-skinned. An octoroon I would think. Very old, with wrinkled hands. She told us how to find this place. You must find her and she will tell you.'

'I am not the examining magistrate. It is sufficient for me that I find you, still grappling with your defenceless victim. There is a clear case for you to answer.'

He nodded to the armed guards, who were following the dialogue without change of expression, as though it was an open and shut case. They took a step forward in concert with the bulbous blasters jutting ahead.

Fletcher had a split second to sort out a policy. Once inside the brig, any kind of charge could be made to stick. The

33

only gunboat in Argentus that could influence events was the Scotian. By the time any I.G.O. detail arrived, they could be long dead with a set of false records that would preclude any reopening of the case and leave a lasting mark of Cain on the European Space office.

On the other hand, any kind of roof-top chase could only end one way. Even if he reached *Callisto,* there was no sanctuary. Port armament could reduce her to trash. A delay at best, with flight making them look guilty as hell.

He let instinct decide it. At that level, the submerged man of action won out. He heard himself speak rapidly to Crowhurst in English, 'Swing towards the bed then back and pitch him for their shoulders.'

Ur-Ilbaba would surely not object to one more contribution to the cause.

At the distance, they could hardly miss. The cadaver hit chest high and fell across the extended arms with enough weight to drop the gun barrels. Charges spat into the floor.

Fergus grabbed for the guard nearest himself and for a count of ten, room sixteen went into spasm like a shaken kaleidoscope.

When the pieces fell into a pattern, Fletcher had a blaster in either hand, one guard was out cold on the deck and the other four were lined up along the rear wall.

Fletcher said, 'You have forced me to take this way. I shall put in a full report to the I.G.O. consulate and to my company. From here, I will go to the space port. But as of now, I want on record the time you came here and the time it is now. Everyone present will sign the document. I shall take the body to the space port medical unit. They will assess the time of death. This will make it clear that death had occurred before our arrival.'

The sub-controller, fairly spitting with anger said, 'Correction, that will only establish that death was before *my* arrival. We do not know precisely when *you* arrived.'

'You will have to find the janitor to establish that. Clearly there would be no point in staying here after the event. Anyway you can have no objection to signing such a document.'

Crowhurst drafted it on a memo pad with a duplicate. When the signatures were at the foot, he tore off the top copy and handed it to the Fingalnan.

Fletcher said, 'I regret that we shall have to make sure that you do not interfere, but as soon as possible I shall inform your office that you are here. If we had been murderers you and your men would now also be dead as a simple means of covering the crime.'

The sub-controller resolutely refused to count his blessings, 'You will have added other serious crimes to your account. Resisting arrest. Assaulting security officers. This will earn you deportation at the least.'

Strips of metal cloth clamped the four mobile guards round the table. The fifth was still out and likely to take time before he was jumping about asking who had done him wrong.

With Ur-Ilbaba rolled in a sheet and drooped over his shoulder, Fletcher led out into the corridor. Next in line, Lorna Diment, tried to keep her eyes off the waltzing Matilda and off the ground at her feet. For her, it was a long five minutes before they were out once more in an empty lobby.

A police tender with a single guard in its pilot seat had drawn up behind *Callisto's* car. He was plainly surprised to see them and full of doubt about what to do for the best.

As they climbed into the car, he solved his dilemma, pulled a short carbine from a roof clip and began to walk over.

Confirmation that a third force had been busy on the site, while they were below ground, came when Fergus thumbed the motor button. The console stayed dead. Even the fault-indicator panel was out.

Lorna Diment's well of libido had filled enough for her to ask, 'And who finds the fault in a fault-finder?'—but the question hung about unanswered.

The Fingalnan guard had reached the hatch and, by a sure instinct, trained his artillery on her sternum. He spoke, however, to Fletcher. 'What do you have in this baggage?'

She opened her mouth to say, 'Do you mind?' but the query had earned a bonanza response which went a long way to undermine the guard's confidence in interrogation as a technique. Fletcher had wedged Ur-Ilbaba into a kerbside seat and obligingly rolled back the covers.

Time had done nothing to smooth the horror from the tortured face and with head and shoulders through the hatch, the guard was barely fifteen centimetres off contact.

It was an open and shut case of ask-a-silly-question. His involuntary recoil disturbed his aim. Fletcher had the carbine by the barrel. Two shots breached the plexidome, then it was free and reversed.

Fletcher said, 'We will join you in your car. You can pilot us to the space port. I want to leave this man with the medical unit.'

Proof that they had taken too long on the outward leg came when the police tender homed on the apron in fifteen minutes dead. Granted, the security blazon had given some advantages in the traffic flow; but it was sure enough that anyone, familiar with the city, could have gotten out to block fifty-three well ahead.

It was evidence that the opposition could think on their feet and mount a military-type operation. Everything pointed to command organization on *Agron*.

Fletcher picked up his long bundle and carried it into the lobby. The Scotian or a dead ringer was standing on the same square metre of terrain. Given his facial geography, he could not look surprised; but he mimed uncertainty. After a two step forward and back shuffle, he stepped out of Tom Tiddler's ground and put himself across the line of march, with a hand on the laser in his belt.

Speech tones were a chore for a palate engineered for a language of a-tonal clicks; but he worked at it and communicated, 'What have you there, Earthman?'

It was a challenge that Fletcher would have been glad to

pass up. He wanted to get to base and regularize the situation without further complication; but he knew that once committed to the enquiry, the Scotian would not let go.

Slowly, he lowered the bale to the deck, where the close wrap of cloth made its contents obvious enough. The Scotian did the sum and confirmed that he knew what it was all about. As Fletcher straightened up, the laser was coming clear of its clip. The Earthman grabbed, two-handed, for the moving wrist and there was a brief explosion of brutality that stopped commerce in the lobby as though caught through a stroboscopic viewer.

For Dag Fletcher, it was a therapy; a release of pent up frustration. In some sense, also, he was working off a first payment for Ur-Ilbaba's death. He took the arm diagonally across his front and brought his knee up in a vicious jab. As the man jacknifed, he let go and chopped definitively into the exposed lizard neck.

The Scotian dropped to the parquet and a surge of sound signalled general release from the spell. A quick-witted clerk at the information desk shoved in an alarm call and an urgent bleep on orchestral A began to echo round the set.

Fletcher picked up his albatross and completed the thirty-metre course to a swing door labelled Medical Centre, as a detachment of port security guards in riot rig with bulbous tranquillizer syringes poking through coffin-lid shields made a spirited sortie from the duty room.

He pushed through the reception pen and was followed into the inner court by a clerk who was getting nowhere with a repeated line, 'Take your turn, the doctor is busy.' Inside, he planked his cadaver on an empty stretcher trolley and whipped off the covering sheet like a master of illusion.

It made a good point. The clerk shut off in mid phrase and a white-coated, elegant, Fingalnan medico, holding a sample tube to a scanning eye, let it fall from her nerveless fingers to the desk top.

Fletcher spoke into the silence, aware that it would not be

with them for long. 'This man has been murdered. I want you to record the time now, and also establish what was the time of death.'

Pounding feet in the outer bailey told him he had cut it fine. He remembered Spencer's stress on the diplomatic nature of the mission and briefly wondered at what point he could have avoided this situation. But it was all water under the bridge. As of now, he was stuck with a small hot war which could only be played one way.

Ur-Ilbaba's migrating Ka—if it was still taking an interest—might well have considered that European Space was still getting service from an old employee.

The incoming posse pulled up short and spent a digestive second sifting the evidence. A brawl in the lobby between foreigners was one thing, this was something else.

It was a delay that lost them the initiative. Fletcher had the carbine in a point blank aim that would take the head off the leading hand. He said, 'That's far enough. Listen. The doctor here is running some tests on this body. Take a few minutes only. After that I want you to take me to Argentus Security H.Q. This man worked for European Space. I want his murderers brought in.'

There was room for compromise in the formula. If he intended to walk into the security strongpoint there was no sense in risking certain casualties to take him to that place.

Professional curiosity clinched the deal.

The doctor walked across to the slab with a diagnostic probe on a wandering lead and shoved its hollow needle tip into Ur-Ilbaba's left leg.

Every eye tracked her back to a desk console where she played an elaborate sequence of permutations on a succession of keys and stops. There was no music, but a small bell rang and the pay-off came in a five centimetre slip of blue tape which she tore off and held up to read.

'He has been dead almost one hour. Fifty-nine point

38

two-three minutes to be precise. He should be sealed at once in a disposal bag.'

Fletcher said, 'That's all I wanted to know. Can I have a copy of that?'

'Certainly.'

When he had the two, he attached one to the first signed statement and handed the file to Crowhurst. The other he gave to the senior guard.

'You saw how that was obtained. You know there is a duplicate in my possession and a permanent record in the computer. Now we can go along to your H.Q.'

To Crowhurst, he said, 'Take our copies back to *Callisto*. Put Halewood in the picture and get him to signal the account to European Space. Lorna and Fergus go with you.'

Crowhurst said, 'I don't like it Commander; once they get you inside there's no telling what framed charge they might pull. I reckon we should take off and wait for the control commission to work on this lot for a while.'

'Look, the only way we can all leave, is by shooting it out. We might just do that; but it leaves them with a cast iron case for refusing a permit to the corporation for good. Just do as I say. I'll be okay.'

Even then, there was doubt that the section leader would go along with it. Fletcher used speech tones. 'My companions will return to the ship. I will go with you now.'

He said stubbornly, 'Not so. You will all come along to H.Q.'

Fletcher took first pressure on the firing stud of the carbine and said evenly, 'On your way, Jim.'

They were touching distance from the two still in the doorway, before the man spoke. A fine silvery sweat had gathered on his forehead. The path of honour was a fine thing; but from the bleak look on the Earthman's face, he reckoned he would be the first to join the majority group of the dead and the nearest example of the genre was no recruiting poster.

He said, 'Let them go.'

Fletcher tried to save his face. 'That was well done, section-leader. There should be no quarrel between us. I am only anxious to reach the truth. Your co-operative attitude will not go unnoticed.'

At the same time, he reversed the carbine and presented it, butt forward.

He was less sure of the long term wisdom of the move, when they dropped into the inner court of the Argentus security block. It was set up like a fortress. There was no force within several light years that could prise him out. He was stuck firmly with the diplomacy bit.

Chapter Three

Administrator Veck was at his usual post by a floor-to-ceiling window overlooking the floodlit centre court, when Fletcher was wheeled in for his seventh audience in thirty-six hours, with nothing to show that this would be any different from the first half dozen.

As on all previous takes, he kept his back to the incoming group of four and waited for the section-leader to cue him in with the formal patter.

'Section-leader, Manishtusu, Excellency. The Earthman, Commander Fletcher, is here, as you requested.'

This time, however, Veck made a change. 'Very good. Leave him. Wait outside. I say, wait outside.'

'And the escort, Excellency?'

'Yes. All outside.'

There was some point in Manishtusu's query. When the hatch closed and Veck turned to his desk, he was seen, in a good light, as small, even by Fingalnan standards and knocking the age range when the ethnic stock went in for a withered frailty that looked deceptively like senile decay.

There was no weakness in his voice, however. It was a quick-fire, high-pitched job, backed by a decade of high office in the security sphere. Behind it, there was a monolithic confidence, that time was on his side and that he had techniques at his elbow to break down any interrogee. Its only gimmick was a tendency to repetition of key phrases as though its owner did not trust the hearer to get the message at one go.

'Commander Fletcher, you see how I am trying to give you every opportunity to state your case. Why will you not co-operate with me? What are we arguing about? The death

41

B*

of this old man is of no importance. There are two hundred murders every week in this city. Mostly confessed and paid for without police intervention. The fine in this case would be less than two hundred international credits. Of course, your other, hasty actions do not help. The court could not overlook them. You must expect deportation. I say, you must expect deportation.'

'When does the case come to court?'

'That is precisely what we are talking about. Until I have your statement of admission there will be no hearing.'

Not for the first time, Fletcher felt that he was in a surrealist sequence where words were counters that changed value with the user.

'You understand that you are acting in direct contravention of the I.G.O. Charter?'

'I would advise you not to concern yourself about the I.G.O. Charter. Fingalna is a sovereign state and has a legal system which antedates anything comparable on your planet by many centuries. I have studied your legal code. It exists to give protection to the criminal. I say, it exists to give protection to the criminal. Here, we believe that law is concerned with protecting the general public.'

'Surely it is also concerned with arriving at the truth of a matter?'

'What is truth? There is factual truth and imaginative truth. Life is more subtle than you suppose.'

'A democratic government must have a system of law, where justice is done and is also seen to be done. Leaving the interpretation to the executive arm has always led to oppression.'

'You use the word "democratic" as though it was a keystone in a coherent system. Other catchwords of your culture are liberty, equality and fraternity. The I.G.O. myth of equality does not mean that in fact all men are equal or indeed that they should receive equal consideration, but that under no circumstances should it be admitted that they are not. There is a great deal of hypocrisy in your charter. Liberty, equality and fraternity are not a cluster, but the points of a triangle. If you approach one you withdraw from the other two. Liberty is two-edged. No government, worthy of the title, can give liberty for the institutions which support it to be undermined.'

'These are interesting issues and although I welcome an opportunity for a philosophical chat, I have work to do. As an I.G.O. travel-pass holder, I want to see or talk to an I.G.O. representative.'

'You still do not know when you are well-off. Nor do you appreciate the situation you are in. Techniques of persuasion are very advanced here. I have only to give the word and you would come to our next meeting with a changed mind. A changed mind.'

'There are documents signed by your own people which confirm the times. Ur-Ilbaba was dead when we arrived. It was known to the Sabazian mining company that we were on the way. They passed the information to the Scotians. A Scotian murdered the old man. The scheme to implicate European Space in an embarrassing episode is childishly obvious.'

'But effective. You speak of documents. Of course, I have them here.'—Veck pressed the top of his desk and a panel whipped away to reveal a shallow tray with Crowhurst's memo and a blue medical tape on a clip.

'Take them and check the times.'

Fletcher went through the motions, though, in a flash of foresight, he realized that he might just as well have saved the energy for whistling a blue tune. The doctor's chit with its estimate of death and time of test was unchanged; but Crowhurst's round robin now showed that they had been surprised, with the body on their hands, fifty-seven minutes before the time the doctor had run the check. That made out that death had been two minutes before the arrival of the sub-

43

controller of the 29th precinct. If true, it was an establishment of guilt.

Fletcher said slowly, 'You know this is false and that I hold the true record?'

'I understand that copies were made and are in your possession. If you have altered them to improve your case, it will not succeed.'

'So, all these interviews and high-minded chat have been organized to give your special effects department time to manufacture this copy. Why go to all this trouble? If you did not want the European Space link, you should have said so. The project was cleared by your Trade Council.'

'You are a very simple man, Commander. Happier, I would think, in a straightforward military situation. I believe it is worthwhile. Let us, for a moment consider your personal position. Although there is no penalty here except a fine and, of course, deportation for what you have done, on your own planet a very different view will be taken. This incident could be the end of your career. I say, it could be the end of your career.'

'Not so. The evidence of my crew will be taken into account. I have three reliable witnesses on the ship. An account of the circumstances will already have gone to I.G.O.'

'As to that, you are ahead of the facts. Your companions did not return to that large, vulgar-looking museum piece. They are in this building. Their future is very much bound up with your attitude and willingness to co-operate.'

Veck paused and let it sink in. Sitting in a high swivel-chair, he could have passed for an automated doll. The hand he stretched out to receive the papers was a parchment skin stretched tautly over bird bones. He went on, 'I could suppress this. Free your crew. Help you to establish your office and underwrite the success of your venture. That would be important to you, would it not?'

'Or?'

'Or I could let affairs take their course. I think, in the

44

interests of a tidy case, it would be better if your three partners were not able to testify. That is no problem. Half an hour in the therapy room and they will remember nothing. Or they could attempt to escape and leave us no alternative but to shoot them.'

'What kind of a deal are you offering?'

'That is a very sensible line to take.'

'Don't take too much for granted, I haven't agreed to a thing.'

'True, but I think you will. I say, I think you will.'

Veck pushed another section of his clever desk and a long console extruded itself like an old-time cinema organ. Courtesy itself, he played the first tune for his guest and a black-cushioned chair whipped up out of the deck at Fletcher's back.

'Sit down Commander. I have something to show you.'

More key work and the house lights dimmed. An actualizer, running from a prepared loop, shoved out a 3-D picture to fill the far end of the oblong room. It was first class equipment. The illusion was complete. They might very well have been there in the flesh.

They were looking down into the piazza of an empty city. The camera crew must have been sited on a high boom. Full colour treatment gave glowing life to brilliant mosaic work and a subtle harmony of tone in the façades of the elegant building blocks that flanked the square.

As the camera panned round, it brought in part of a high fly-over on tall striding arches with the balance of mass and strength refined to the ultimate milligramme. It was clear now that the whole city was set underground in a vast, domed cavern.

As the viewing eye moved on, Fletcher knew what was coming next. The angle was new, but the scene was fixed in his holographic memory for all time. There was the armed scout car, which had met him as he broke through the last, white barrier.

Something of the tension of that suicide bid, had him

45

gripping the arms of his chair. And then briefly, he saw *Petel's* tiny scout car whip out of the tunnel mouth, with its I.G.O. pennant streaming straight back, firing a brilliant line of heavy-calibre laser into the waiting Fingalnan. That was Bennett, who died there, and Quilliam in the pilot slot taking them up in a crazy roll that flung them out of the picture.

Fletcher said, 'I did not know there was a record. Taken from the ship, of course. It was a military action. Our planets were on different sides.'

'I understand that. It is not held against you. You do not need to make excuses.'

'I do not make excuses. But this would be a reason for your attitude. A kind of revenge.'

'Not so. Compromising one man would be small recompense for the loss of a supership and many of our best soldiers. You remember the affair then?'

'Of course. It was on Plantos Three. Your ship was hidden in the main square of one of the underground cities. Shortly after that sequence, it was destroyed.'

'Destroyed?'

'The scout car was crash-dived at one of the tripod jacks. The ship fell into the square. Later, we placed charges to break up the hulk.'

'And the wreckage remains in the square?'

'That is so. It will stay there for centuries, preserved like that ancient city. But what is your interest in a remote skirmish? Your own officers were returned and, as far as I know, are still alive.'

'That is so. Admiral Xantu is here in Argentus. He supplied the piece of film. I say, he supplied the piece of film.'

There was silence. Fletcher was away on another line of thought. Some of the emotional content of the time in the square had flooded back. He remembered the crowded sequence when Quilliam had shot the ejector, just before the car had homed on its target. He had come down on the

46

piazza in a state of shock with debris crashing round him and the ship coming down like a falling tower.

He could see the floor, vivid as an eidetic image. There was the picture of a girl; dark hair, head back, eyes like black milk. Across the gap of time, she had sparked off a will to live and got him moving out from under with centimetres to spare.

It took a positive effort of will to bring himself back to the quiet room. Whatever effect Veck had intended, there was one which could not be in his favour. Fletcher was out of diplomacy. He was back in a military role and was already moving round the desk to grab the administrator as the handiest hostage to fortune.

Veck showed that age had not withered all his reflexes. He moved urgently and shoved down a stud. Fletcher's grabbing hands hit an invisible power screen like a plate glass shutter and the jar numbed his arms to the shoulder.

It was an acoustic barrier too; but Veck's mime was unmistakable. Plainly enough, it told him to get back to his seat and cool off.

There was, in fact, no other profitable angle. Veck and his box of tricks were inviolable. After a single turn round the room, Fletcher did just that and waited bitterly for the next transmission.

When it came, it was against all expectation and he could not pretend to understand any part of it.

'Your company is setting up an agency. One of the services you offer is that of charter flights. I hope the craft involved will be more up-to-date than the ship you have used to come here. Are you, yourself, available to pilot a ship on charter?'

It was a complete change of direction and no doubt there was something behind it that should give him pause; but in the absence of any other guide line, he took it straight, at face value.

'Eventually that is so. But first I have to establish the

terminal. We need staff, equipment, regular use of space at the port. This will take time. I could not offer a ship for several months.'

'Suppose I was to give you help, so that these preliminaries could be shortened?'

'Then it would be sooner. But why should you do that? So far, there has not been much co-operation. Also, if you have urgent need of a charter your own national service could provide it.'

'That is not easy. The control commission restricted our fleet and has fixed limits on the areas in which it can operate.'

Light dawned belatedly. Fletcher said, 'Hold it there. If you want European Space to break I.G.O. regulations, you're out of luck.'

'Not so. What I have in mind is neither a trading mission, nor one with any infringement of traffic regulations. Not, that is, for an Earth-registered ship. The voyage is off limits only for a Fingalnan vessel and crew. I should remind you that you are not well placed to refuse.'

'So that was the point of the exercise.'

'Shall I go on?'

'After all your trouble, you might as well.'

'You saw the film. You could pilot a ship to Plantos Three and find the wreck of *Leviathon*. As you know, she was the flagship of the Fingalnan fleet. When she escaped, she was, in a sense, the paymaster of the force. She was carrying a very large sum in negotiable securities, which was destined for one of the allied governments. It is Fingalnan money. Legally sound. If it was known to be there, it would be an Eldorado for unscrupulous adventurers and its misuse could undermine our economy.'

'But you tell me.'

'You are in a special case. I can erase the knowledge or make sure that you are in no position to communicate anything.'

'What is the proposition?'

48

'A simple one. That you pilot a ship to Plantos Three and recover *Leviathon's* safe. A confidential mission, you understand, which you reveal no one for obvious reasons. I say, for obvious reasons.'

When it was out and said, Fletcher marvelled at his own simplicity. This was a very subtle piece of organization. It must have been planned from the minute the crew manifest of *Callisto* had been signalled through to Argentus and his own name had been spotted by some busy-minded bastard.

Where did he stand then? On the face of it, there was not much wrong with it, except the method. It was a mission he might well have accepted as a straightforward proposition to get the agency off to a flying start. The I.G.O. control commission was concerned with a lasting peace, it had no interest in knocking the Fingalnan economy.

On the other hand, it was a bad move to start the agency under duress. Gratitude on either side could turn sour.

Veck's bright, beady eyes had never left Fletcher's face. There was no doubt, he thought it was all over bar the shouting. For the first time, he tried a more persuasive tone and came near to spoiling his case. 'Now you see Commander, we can be generous. I say, we can be generous. You have a fine record and I know you would be exactly the right man for this mission. As an earnest of the co-operation you can expect, I have had your office cleared and refurnished. It will be ready for occupation whenever you like and staff will be provided.'

It sounded a warning note in Fletcher's head. The man was too sure of himself and too keen altogether to push the thing along. There were other space lines. Even the Scotian could have been briefed for this. Except that many of the traditional contacts were also under restriction and no one but a fool would trust a Scotian as far as he could throw a lead pig.

Instinct was moving him to say no. His mouth was opening to tell Veck that there was no deal, when a now familiar rush of imagery to the head sent the room in a slow spin.

'Are you ill, Commander? I say, are you ill?'

Veck's hand was on a summoning stud when Fletcher's eyes cleared. He said thickly, 'That's all right, Administrator. Not to worry. A dizzy spell. Eyestrain more than likely.'

At the same time, he was grappling with a third force in the symposium. For whatever reason, Hulda was trying to influence him. There was no explicit verbal logic about it; but an unmistakable weight on one arm of the seesaw. She wanted him to accept. More than that, there was an urgent *requirement* that he should accept. When he began to speak, the pass was already sold.

Fletcher said, 'I believe you have gone the wrong way about this proposition. But now you have gotten to framing it, I see nothing against it. There may be a time lag before I can organize a ship; but you do your part and I'll do mine. You have a deal.'

'I am delighted that we now see eye to eye, Commander. You will be prepared to sign an agreement.'

The entente suffered a small setback as Fletcher asked, 'Is that important? With your organization, documents of any kind are no problem. I have agreed, that is binding on my side.'

Veck considered it. 'Very well. Again, I must emphasize the delicate nature of the mission. I have been frank with you, but when the charter is set up, the object will not appear on the manifest. It will be to ferry a trading delegation to Cappodan and the detour to Plantos will be off record. Only you and I know the precise nature of this business. It must not be revealed to any of your associates.'

'The crew will have to know.'

'Not until you are well on the journey. After the event, it is not important. We shall say nothing and it will be in your interest to keep the matter quiet, since it involves what might be regarded in some quarters as a breach of regulations. There is another matter also. We have many trained space personnel made redundant by the temporary reduction in our fleets. A proportion of Fingalnan crewmen must be included. This is a regular feature of charter procedures. I say, this is a regular feature of charter procedures.'

Fletcher thought, 'The old fox, he surely has it all buttoned up.' But having conceded the main issue, he was not one to strain at trifles.

'Very well. Now let me see my staff. It all depends on you.'

Certainly, there could be no grouch about the way Veck handled his side of the deal. At the end of a week, Trudy Brogan was calling European Space with a run down of progress that had Spencer calling back within the hour.

'What's all this, Fletcher? What in the name of god have you been spending?'

'Very little, Chairman. The Fingalnans want the link and they're being very co-operative. You got my urgent memo on the charter?'

'I did and I regret that we can't meet it. Not for two months at least. You know we didn't expect to move at this pace.'

'That's bad. They want that service. They've been restricted as you know; I made a promise there.'

'Well you should know better. I can't whistle a multi-million piece of equipment out of the air. Use *Callisto,* she's sound enough.'

'I'll have to. Meanwhile you can pick a manager for this end and get him out here. I'll be finished with phase one in a couple of weeks.'

Spencer said suspiciously, 'What have you been up to? I just don't believe in altruism. What have you sold them?'

It was a question that Fletcher was asking himself.

Hulda and the I.G.O. staff were settled in a composite office and living suite across the square, but he had not seen her alone since his release from the brig.

In company, she had avoided all reference to the charter

decision and he was beginning to think that he had imagined her intervention. It could have been his own mind, finding a scapegoat or a reason to accept something which was expedient.

Veck took the news of the choice between delay or accepting *Callisto* as a piece of diplomatic hedging.

'Have I not carried out my part of the agreement, Commander? Is there anything else you want? I say, is there anything else you want?'

'Look, I told you there might be a time lag. I'm prepared to use *Callisto*. She's a good ship. There's no problem.'

But Veck had clearly been briefed in detail by someone with a professional knowledge of spacecraft and it occurred to Fletcher that the *éminence grise* in the equation was probably Xantu himself.

'Navigation to Plantos is not easy and the entry to the underground hangar requires a small, powerful ship with a high power ratio. I have a further suggestion which should be acceptable to your company.'

'Which is?'

'Those units of the military fleet which were on Fingalnan soil at the armistice were disarmed and returned to our ownership. They have not been brought into civilian service, because, as you will appreciate, they are not easily adapted for freight purposes. There is a K class corvette, however, which was partially converted for use as a government shuttle to transport trade delegations. This could be released to your company for a nominal sum. It would be useful to you as the nucleus of your fleet based on Argentus. Once registered in your name, we could use it for this charter. Indeed, considering the charter fee, which could be offset against the price, you would get a very good bargain. I say, you would get a very good bargain.'

Fletcher believed it without the repetition. When he inspected the corvette, he was more than ever convinced. *Konstet* was almost new. She had been finished during the war and had flown only one mission after her trials. She was a worthwhile acquisition for any fleet.

He made an urgent call to European Space. Spencer said, 'I don't know what's going on there. You must be using some kind of cunning, devilish necromancy. I'll release the funds right away. Remind me never to talk to you without a lawyer, I don't want to find I've signed the corporation over to you.'

Among his own staff, there was a similar attitude of doubtful amazement.

Talking to Crowhurst in the luxury office, Lorna Diment put the question in words. 'How did he do it, Jim? We were at a dead end. They had it all buttoned up. What did he say to that loopy mandarin to get us off of the hook?'

Halewood was more direct, he said, 'I don't like it Dag. Things are going too well. After getting you all set up, he turns into a Dutch uncle. What's in it for them?'

They were on their way to the military port a hundred kilometres north of Argentus to collect the corvette. Fletcher had taken the three executives with Fergus to pilot the car and every head turned his way to hear the answer.

So far, he had kept the detail to himself, but he reckoned this was a good time to talk it out. They were following an old surface road which ran straight as a scored line over a relief map of bland, silver downs. He said, 'Put us down, Fergus. Anywhere here, just off the road.'

When the car stopped, he motioned for all out and took them fifty metres into the bush, feeling like a Hebrew prophet off to the mountains for a tablet. Though Trudy Brogan in a brilliant red leotard was an unlikely camp follower for a seer at that.

He said, 'I'm doubtful about any place we have. Even *Callisto* is probably on a listening beam by this time. Not that I have a lot to say, but what there is, I want to be private. I'll tell you I made a deal with Veck, to get progress. I'll take full responsibility for it and to be fair to the man, I can't tell you, at this stage, what the small print says. But to be fair to you, it concerns the charter flight to Cappodan. Now I shall need a rep from each section to work with experienced Fingalnan crew. This makes sense, because it leaves *Callisto* operational. That cuts you out, Gary. In my absence, you take charge. For the rest, I want you to put it discreetly to your section and get a genuine volunteer. I'm sorry, but that's as far as I can go.'

Galloway said, 'I'll not be bothering my boys. You can take it now, Commander, that I'll go along.'

'If you take six Fingalnans, they'll be the majority party'— Bramah had no opinion of any other ethnic group as space-crew.

'So? It's their charter. There's no point in hi-jacking *Konstet* if that's what you mean.'

'No, I suppose not. I just mention it. But I'll be happy to come along. I've had too much of Argentus.'

Trudy Brogan said, 'You can count me in. Mercer can take over on *Callisto*.'

'Well, that's settled then. Except that I'd like two in the power section. That's where we might meet problems with an unfamiliar craft. What about you, Fergus?'

There was no doubt about the reaction. On any audience response meter, Fergus would have clocked a surge.

The wisdom of having two power specialists was clear when Fletcher took *Konstet* off the pad for a trial orbit of Fingalna before taking her in to the terminal now allocated to European Space at Argentus.

She was big for a corvette, knocking the lower limits of frigate specification, with a mass of ancillary gear that gave fine handling for a combat role, but was well in excess of the needs of a civilian craft. Remembering the tricky navigation required on the dark side of Plantos Three, Fletcher reckoned he had been lucky. *Callisto* would have done the job, at full stretch with no margin for human error. This one would make it easy, even with a mixed crew.

For that matter, he had no complaints with the seven

54

Fingalnans allocated by the military base. They were sealed up ready and waiting in the ship when he arrived and his first contacts were by voice on the intercom.

All were English-speaking which was an immediate gain. Controls were pictographed for international use. It was all too easy.

Konstet handled well. Coming in to Argentus, he took it on manual. Partly as a public relations exercise to show the new men that they were working with an expert and partly to test their reactions to a piece of basic navigation.

It was a copy-book exercise. The co-pilot, answering to Gimel-Sin, was no conversationalist. Unusual for a Fingalnan, he kept commands to a curt minimum. Response from his compatriots was, however, prompt and even deferential. When *Konstet* blazed down on her pad, in a flare of finely-calculated retro, there was no doubt in Fletcher's mind that from the technical point of view, the mission was in the bag.

Complications, when they came, were from his own side of the fence. Sarpedon called in the office, filling the door frame of the inner interview room with his sombre bulk and opening with a direct statement that was difficult to duck.

'Commander Fletcher, I am not happy about this charter. I would like your assurance that it does not contravene the control commission's restrictions.'

'You have the manifest. It is a trade delegation to Cappodan. There is a traditional link between the two planets which was suspended during the war years.'

'That I know, of course, what I also know is that the three delegates are or have been military personnel. A curious choice you will agree.'

'That surely is their business. I take them and bring them back. What they do there is not my concern.'

'But it is mine. I think that one of my staff should accompany you.'

Conscious that in all probability the conversation was being monitored, and asking himself where Hulda fitted in with

55

this seemingly straightforward request, Fletcher said, 'That would be difficult, Commissar. Accommodation is already strained. *Konstet* is not fully converted for civil use. Surely the voyage is unimportant. If you feel that surveillance is necessary, the I.G.O. consulate in Cappodan could be alerted.'

'That is so. I am aware of that possibility. You are unable to take another passenger?'

'Correct.'

'Very well.' Sarpedon heaved his frame off the visitor's chair and treated his host to a straight and considering look. 'You have nothing to add to fill out our information on this charter?'

'Nothing that is of any importance to I.G.O.'

'I trust that, with your experience of I.G.O. work, you can assess that.'

'Only time will tell.'

'As you say, only time will tell. When do you leave?'

'1650 hours tomorrow.'

'Your course is agreed by my office?'

'Yes.'

'Then I hope you will have an uneventful journey.'

When he had gone, Dag Fletcher sat back and considered it. The facts did not add up.

Unless he had imagined Hulda's intervention, she was aware of what was intended and must have had reason to support it. Had she or had she not shared that with her chief? Also Sarpedon could have recorded their recent conversation. Very likely had done. At a later enquiry, it could be played back with damaging effect. He could imagine a court looking at him as his own voice condemned him. Some snide lawyer making a big play with it. 'But at that very time Commander Fletcher, you *knew* that a detour was planned. You deliberately concealed the knowledge from the Commissar. In fact you positively *denied* that any breach of regulation was intended. What kind of action is that for a man in a position of trust?'

And the reason would bring contempt. Basically, because he

56

was being blackmailed to save his own skin and to cover up an unsavoury murder case.

Action was a relief. At least, he knew what he was doing in the ship. There was a good feel about the controls. The Fingalnans were inspired imitators. Every refinement thought up by every other spacefaring planet had been incorporated in *Konstet,* with that additional flair for micro gear which was their special hallmark.

By 1600, he was satisfied that he could pilot her in blindfold. He had kept the crew at stations for two hours, until there was no permutation of executive command that was not understood by all hands.

He ordered a twenty-minute stand easy and flipped out the seals of his suit to make a final tour unhampered.

The trade delegation was housed in the main gunnery control centre below the cone and as he stepped through the hatch, he went back in time to military service, when he had gone the rounds in a fighting ship. Acceleration couches were unmodified. The three Fingalnans with visors tripped back looked very much at home.

Conversation stopped as he came in, one of them had swung out a fire bar with its miniature console, so that he looked like a gunner taking a spell between engagements. He fitted the role, too. By the nudge of a sixth sense, Fletcher knew the man had used that equipment before.

Confirmation came on the fifth day out, with *Konstet* running like a clockwork bobbin on the long thread spun by its own computers.

Fletcher came fully awake, like a cat, on the first bleep of the tell-tale in his cabin roof. The sitrep showed that a ship had been picked up on a converging course with a half-hour to run before the projections would cross.

When he reached the command island, Gimel-Sin was already there, fully sealed up and taking reports from the sections.

57

Checking round his console, Fletcher saw a cluster glowing redly with the all-systems-go signal which he had not expected to see again.

It was the gunnery control quadrant and if telling no lie, was putting enough destructive power to devastate a continent in the span of his left thumb.

Chapter Four

Dag Fletcher took a long minute to consider the phenomenon. One way and another, the enterprise was escalating out of all proportion from the near-innocent proposition originally put by Veck. He considered where, if anywhere, along the line he could have called a halt and came to the conclusion, like Macbeth, that he had stepped so far in blood that he was equidistant from either shore.

It rankled, that Veck and whoever was behind Veck, were thinking with some justification that he was simple. A mere lyre for their plucking fingers. Well, it had gone far enough. When the documents were in the ship's safe, he would alert Spencer and get I.G.O. advice. If there was no more to it than Veck had said, then it would be cleared. If not the whole business could be brought into daylight. Come to think, his position was strengthened by the Fingalnan initiative in this mission. Veck could hardly pretend that a criminal charge was known to lie against the man he had employed on a confidential enterprise.

His minute had brought the distant ship from a hurrying silver speck to an identifiable shape on the main scanner. It was enough to dispel the smog of self doubt and make him glad to see the red glow on his console. There was another non-civilian element on his spread. Its use would surprise his own crew more than the rest, but would be a final showdown for the Fingalnans. Its pictograph showed the stylized representation of a rocket ship with every turret spitting flame. When he shoved it over, a keening wail sirened through the ship and a bright legend in Fingalnan appeared as an inset on every scanner. At the same time, he said, 'Break out the I.G.O. pennant.'

Trudy Brogan, the linguist read it off for all doubters. 'Clear for Action.' Then she repeated it as a question, not having volunteered for any draft. 'Clear for *action?* What goes on? Clear what? Request amplification of this signal.'

Reaction from the Fingalnans was precise and matter of fact. From the gunnery cabin a clipped, metallic voice said, 'Main armament, all systems go.'

The approaching ship had doubled in size. It was a five centimetre cylinder; a small deadly projectile; wasp-waisted, showing the black and yellow markings of a Scotian. Not *Agron* for a sure thing; no standard space craft that he knew could have come up from that quarter after making a later start from the same pad.

What would a Scotian be after? On the face of it, there was an alliance with Fingalna. So she could be coming in to help the Fingalnan crew to take over the ship. But then an alliance was of no importance to Scotia. She was as dangerous as an ally as a declared enemy. Whatever suited the logic of the minute was her style, and if the rumour of easy money on *Leviathon* had got around, it would not matter who the owner was.

Either way, he was pig-in-the-middle.

Fletcher took one of the most unpalatable decisions of his career; but he reckoned that if he was going to fight the ship, he needed experts at every console. He said, 'Commander to all sections. Executives stand down. Keep watching brief and assist where necessary. Number One, choose your men to take each section. Quick now.'

To some extent, it was proof that the Fingalnans were not in on the new development. Gimel-Sin wasted no time. He said, 'Navigation, Lurdak. Communications, Furvil. Power, Sondet. All have served in a ship of this class, in action, Commander. All are executive rank. Be assured you have full backing.'

Fletcher said, 'Major course change,' and took *Konstet* on manual. Already, he had given the Scotian too long to pace them and beam onto their navigational computers. Only a completely random move could break the revealed flight pattern.

Random it was and Furvil was stretched to the limit of expertise in keeping a picture of the Scotian centred in the main scanner.

Fletcher dropped in an equilateral spiral that threatened to take *Konstet* up her own streaming rocket tubes. Then he pulled out at a crazy turn that took his crew to the limit of G. tolerance. Every metre of the way, he was working over towards the approaching ship.

Now it was a thousand kilometres distant, within easy speaking range and had still made no challenge.

Fletcher took the initiative, calling in speech tones, 'What ship is that?'

There was no answer, but the scanner was bringing up more detail. The name at the waist had been blanked. Flexible grabs were shoved out fore and aft from their housings. Intention was clearly to board *Konstet*.

That figured, if they knew the general aim of the mission, they would not know all the detail. They would need a few survivors to work over to get chapter and verse.

Fletcher called again. 'This is the European Space Corporation ship *Konstet,* navigating under I.G.O. licence. Keep off.'

As if in answer, the Scotian made a first course change since she had been sighted. It was a turn that *Konstet* might have copied, but which her crew could not have endured. Fletcher could imagine the packed decks of the other ship. Scotians carried twice the personnel of normal craft. On long voyages, they could survive with little food or water in a kind of reptilian hibernation. Their sluggish blood would hardly stir in a centrifuge. Now, lying like so many human torpedoes, they would take any strain that aerobatics could demand.

For a brief count, Fletcher had a blank scanner. Then

61

Furvil picked up a picture. The distance was halved and the raider was coming on like a demented corkscrew.

Fletcher was calling for an estimate of the course and Trudy Brogan threw it on a subsidiary scanner like a bright solenoid. It was a familiar avoidance pattern. On that tack, it would be impossible to hit. His mind grappled with vectors and times. What the Scotian was doing was good, but over predictable. Maybe, he was unaware that he was dealing with an armed ship.

Fletcher lined *Konstet* up for an arrow thrust down the coil. Distance halved and halved again and he set *Konstet* in a slow spin to match the full circling turns of the Scotian. There would be a single non-recurring instant, when *Konstet's* main armament would bear and he called the gunnery cabin to give him the control on remote.

A second's hesitation took them nearer by two hundred kilometres and Gimel-Sin said, 'Do that, gunner.'

It was an interesting side light on the situation, but there was no time to analyse the implications. As the firing pin glowed green, there was a jar that rattled every plate in the hull. The Scotian had sent a burst of small fire raking along the tail. A warning shot that meant heave-to, in any language.

Fletcher was integrated with the machinery, knowing his own reaction time to a nonasecond and working a vein of intuition that bounced out like personal radar, he shoved down the firing pin as *Konstet* came round.

The ship lurched bodily off course as the main armament delivered and corrective jets fired to stabilize. For a count of three, there was enough to do for all hands to stop her wheeling, base over cone, in a destructive wheel of flame.

When she levelled off, the Scotian was too distant to be seen in the direct vision ports. Furvil, working with frenetic speed interpolated from his last fix and pulled a picture out of the void. He was only just in time, at that. The Scotian was neatly sheared through its centre section and the two halves were withdrawing from each other like fragments of an exploded star, with a half dozen small figures and a raft of debris still waiting for the logic of mechanics to dictate which trail to follow after.

Fletcher said, 'Major course change,' and mounting G sank them to the limits of their acceleration couches as he brought *Konstet* back to her original course.

Furvil lost his fix and the screens went blank. Except for the subjective knowledge that it had taken place, the action might never have been.

Sections reported damage. They had been lucky. There was no major penetration of the hull. But Fletcher wrapped it up by a standard check procedure. 'Number One, take a party out and make good. Stand down. Cruising watch.'

He got one incredulous response. Trudy Brogan, shaken out of professional calm, said, 'Commander. You're not *leaving* them? We must go and pick up survivors.'

'They'll be dead. Either when that ship split, or as soon as they found themselves in space. It's a Scotian drill. They're never taken alive. Don't waste your pity on them, they have no human emotions.'

He might have added, 'Except a liking for warm-blooded females.' If it had gone the other way, she would have been more vulnerable than any of them. It now looked as though the mission was going to be anything but straightforward. He would have been better to leave his civilian crew out of it altogether. Since he was the one who had made the deal, he ought to have carried the can alone.

Speculation cut off as Gimel-Sin said, 'Congratulations, Commander, that was a very fine piece of navigation. I am sorry I could not inform you earlier that the ship is armed; but you can see that it is necessary.'

'As to that, I shall have more to say, hereafter; but, as of now, you have a point. How did they know?'

'That is what I am asking myself. Though, since the war, there have been a number of Scotian ships on independent piratical ventures. It could be one of those.'

63

It was not convincing. Fletcher said, 'Do you understand the statistical probability of any ship intercepting our course without prior knowledge?'

'I appreciate that. It is most unlikely. We must assume that the object of the mission is known. In that event, I suggest that we alter course and approach Plantos from a different vector.'

'I'll think about it.'

More than an hour of the exercise produced nothing good. He came round again and again to the view that *Agron* must have whistled up the interceptor. In which case, a great deal must be known about the journey.

Very likely the ship would have signalled that she was closing on her quarry. A blank after that, and it would not take too long to piece together an explanation. Another craft would be brought up. Maybe others had already been alerted to make straight for the Plantos area in case the interception misfired. They could not expect to win again. Next time, it would be known that *Konstet* had teeth and another commander would be more wary.

He was still debating it, when the 'All Stations' call went again. This time, he was in his seat on the command island before Gimel-Sin had arrived and took the first report himself.

Bramah had picked up an etiolated bleep, which could be a ship or could be a small asteroid. It was approaching on a course which could have brought it from Fingalna at a rate which almost ensured it was not a ship. Not the quarter for another Scotian either. But other O.G.A. units could be involved. Honour among thieves was a myth. Any one of the O.G.A. allies would go for its own ends given half a chance.

Fletcher thought, 'Perhaps I can do it one more time. Then there will be another and another. Eventually, we have to miss and it's all over.'

Now Furvil was bringing it in and there was no longer any doubt. It was a small, express sloop. One of the latest

I.G.O. communications craft. Unarmed. Built solely for speed, with a huge power pack and narrow accommodation for two crew and a passenger.

Konstet could disperse her as molecular trash if she came within range.

Gunnery control said, unasked, 'On target. Ready to fire.'

Fletcher called sharply, 'Hold fast,' and shoved the remote fire control out of circuit. Then he called for half speed.

A voice using speech tones sounded through the tannoy. 'I.G.O. sloop *Pegasus*. Urgent memo for Commander Fletcher. Request permission to come aboard.'

For the first time, Gimel-Sin was out of key with the command decision. In his book, there was almost as much to be feared from I.G.O. interference as from the Scotian. His hand snaked out to reconnect the gunnery cabin and got no farther than the edge of the console, where it was pinned flat.

Fletcher said, 'That's far enough, Number One. This is the law, not a pirate. Signal "message understood" and run out a landing mat from number three hatch.'

With his free hand, he fished in the pocket beside his couch and brought out a small, compact laser. Then he went on, 'Make no mistake. Any non-co-operative move on your part and you will fetch up with a hole in your head.'

The wait for *Pegasus* to come alongside brought a slow build of tension that was tangible even in the insulation of a space suit.

The 'action stations' call had brought all hands except Fergus and the three pseudo-economists into the control cabin. They were packed like wheel spokes round the command island and Fletcher circled slowly to check for any sudden movement, conscious that at all times his back was towards a Fingalnan.

But it was clear that any hostile act would execute the co-pilot and there was exemplary caution all round. In any event, they had it made. He could not stay there for ever and

65

the incoming official would be vulnerable as soon as he stepped over the sill.

Pegasus appeared in a direct vision port and sidled up to the hatch. Flexible grabs whipped out to hold her steady and there was a pause as her party worked through their own pressure lock. Two bulky figures stepped on to the mat and clawed a way over.

Galloway reported formally, 'Number three lock open now, Commander.'

The newcomers would think it strange that no one should be detailed to meet them. Fletcher called Fergus, who was on a lonely stint at the emergency power console, below the collision bulkhead, 'John. Get along to Number three and take them along to my cabin.'

Excluding the gunnery control from the general net, he said, 'Hear this, I'm going along to see what they want. As far as I am concerned, part of this mission is still confidential. But I will not directly oppose an authorized I.G.O. official. You'll have to take that on trust. Galloway, catch this laser. If you have any trouble shoot the co-pilot first. Don't hesitate. Do you understand?'

'I ken fine. It'll be a rare pleasure.'

Fletcher shot back his clips and picked his way across the crowded floor. Only heads could move, but they tracked round after him like so many animated footballs.

Outside, he tipped back his visor and found that a faint pollen cloud in the companion brought a new dimension to the set. One of the boarding party was female and familiar at that.

His own cabin was as crowded for its size as the control room. Fergus was standing by the door. Inside, a dark, unknown man in his middle forties, who yet seemed to be looking at him as though he expected to be recognized, was standing by the table and Hulda, for want of anywhere to put her feet was sitting with her knees up on the bed.

His first reaction was that he ought to have known that

she was near. It was a thought which she easily intercepted and answered aloud, 'I was not sure how popular I would be as a passenger, so I thought we would surprise you.'

'You surprise me, all right. What is this, hitching a ride to Cappodan?'

'Not quite that. This is someone you know. Commodore Simpson. He will tell you all about it.'

'Simpson?'—Now memory turned its blind corner— 'Simpson. Commander out of *Falcon*. You look older than you should.'

'That's a fine thing to say. It shows who does all the work. Not everybody lands on a soft civilian billet.'

Simpson had been one of the toughest corvette commanders in Varley's squadron. A professional soldier on a long-term engagement. Commodore. That meant he had left corvettes and gone into the small executive group that handled all the missions for the Earth planet detachment of the I.G.O. fleet. A top brass messenger.

Simpson went on: 'The squadron is in the area and Varley dropped into Argentus with a detachment to answer an I.G.O. call, the day after you left. As soon as he got the score, he sent me out to contact you. Now I know you wouldn't go against the I.G.O. interest. So does Varley. He sends you his regards, by the way; but we can't quite follow this piece of commercial jiggery-pokery.'

'But you didn't come all this way just to say that. This forked stick bit went out a long time ago. There is radio.'

'You're right. Can we talk here?'

'I don't suppose so. I would say that every part of this ship is wired for sound. But I can see that what we say does not get transmitted outside, if that helps.'

'It doesn't. I'll say nothing at this stage, except that you've got an additional two passengers along. I'd like to see what goes on from a military point of view and this bed ornament is in it for the political angle.'

Even in a space suit, the angle she was holding had a nonpolitical bias—gauntleted fingers linked round her knees, pale hair in a complicated swathe topped by a knot of black *chiffon* to hold it steady under the visor which was currently hinged back.

Fletcher thought, irritably, 'God, she communicates freely enough when I don't want to know. Why doesn't she let me in on the big secret now? Not even a very refined bug could get in on that line.'

All he got, however, was open speech, with every appearance of a frank confession.

'Sarpedon called in the patrol, because there are reports of O.G.A. ships being sighted. It may be nothing, but he thought it would do no harm to show the flag. I want a quick passage to Cappodan for a talk with the commissar there. Envoy extraordinary, you might say.'

Suave Simpson, who never missed a trick, said, 'Extra-ordinary is right. You are the most luscious commissar in the service.'

The word 'Yuk' appeared in banner headlines in Fletcher's head. So she could work the transfer, if she wanted. The sentiment was okay; but it annoyed him to be on the receiving end of hand-outs like a poor relation. He said, 'Before you all get too enthusiastic about the trip, there are some things you should know. *Pegasus* was within a fraction of being crisped. This ship is armed. A condition I only discovered *after* blast off. You'll just have to believe that. Now I have given an undertaking, for reasons that I can't go into in detail, to make a small detour and pick up a piece of Fingalnan property from a wreck. My judgement is that it is not against I.G.O. interest; but I will concede that it does not figure on the charter. That said, you are welcome to come along.'

'Detour where?'—Something in Simpson's tone made Fletcher suspect that it was only for confirmation. He already knew the answer.

'Plantos. Plantos Three. You know the situation, you were

in the action with *Falcon*. The wreck of *Leviathon*.'

Agreement again was a shade too ready. 'That's okay. It only adds a few days to the round trip. Signal *Pegasus* to return to base.'

'One more thing. I have seven Fingalnan crew and three so-called trade specialists. All serving military personnel, I would guess. At the moment, one of my own men is holding a gun on the co-pilot. They were not keen to let you on board.'

'Then an extra watch-keeping officer will be useful. The commissar can beguile them by doing a little dance from time to time.'

Fletcher thought it out. If there was any long negotiation with the sloop, it would provoke the Fingalnans to take action. Presented with a *fait accompli,* they would have to accept the situation.

He flicked the intercom for direct speech with the communications desk. 'Trudy. Signal the sloop. Two passengers are staying aboard. She can go home.'

They heard a muted relay on the tannoy and then the sloop crossed a direct vision port making a spectacular turn in its own length.

Simpson said, 'He could have taken a memo back.'

'Not a chance. I want to clear up this mission and finish with it. I don't want the squadron appearing on Plantos.'

'I only hope you know what you're doing.'

'It would be a wise man who knew that.'

Hulda had spent the time wriggling out of her chrysalis and stood revealed in a plain, delphinium inner suit like a Matisse nude. She said, 'You have one female on the crew list then? Perhaps she would lend me something to wear?'

Simpson plugged at it, 'Don't give it a thought, Commissar. You have a plain duty to spread psychological uplift. Well, uplift.'

Thinking that she was manifestly in need of none, herself, Fletcher earned himself an unspoken rebuke, by being cut dead as she walked first through the hatch with her suit over her arm. He reckoned it was a little hard on a man, when his thoughts were not his own. She would be a hard one to surprise with a compliment or in any other way, for that matter.

This second gloss, got him an answer which must have puzzled Simpson as the non-sequitur of all time.

'You will just have to try that much harder, Commander.'

In the control room, the tableau was as he had left it. The civilian element had tipped back their visors. It was another indicator of the military ambience that surrounded the Fingalnans, they were waiting for somebody to call off the emergency.

Fletcher gathered in his laser and spoke on the general net. 'We have two extra personnel along for the trip. It makes no difference to the agreement I made on this charter.

'Commodore Simpson is on passage to Cappodan and will use my cabin, taking alternate command watch in the pilot chair. I.G.O. Commissar Hulda will have a similar arrangement with Executive Brogan. Resume normal speed and course for Plantos. Stand down in five minutes.'

Less than twenty-four hours convinced Fletcher that the additions to his manifest were almost all gain.

He had never known Simpson well and basically found the man an antipathetic type. But there was no doubt about his value as a seasoned spaceman and, in small doses, his bonhomie was good for morale. Also Fletcher realized that his own party would have been under strain, now that the Fingalnans had shown that they were ready to buck any unpopular command decision.

Bramah, Fergus, Galloway, Simpson and himself divided the day in a continuous watch, though there was no sign that any fresh take-over bid was intended. *Konstet* settled into routine and reeled back distance, until on the fifth day from the arrival of the sloop, the complex gravisphere of the Plantos group showed up as a measurable force.

Plantos Three was a dark dime-sized blue on the main scanner, when he warped out of rationalized time and called a conference in the small wardroom.

Gimel-Sin and Sondet—the Power Two—represented the chartering party. Fletcher had Simpson, Bramah, and Galloway to listen to his presentation of the facts. With Hulda, on request, for interest.

'We have a choice of procedure. Plantos is a dead planet. One side is permanently dark and navigation is tricky. Finding the entrance to the underground complex would be difficult and it will now be under a thick layer of ice. I know the location within a square kilometre; but landmarks are confusing. We could spend a month sorting it out.

'Last time, we made our entry from one of the radial tunnel systems. Once inside, you can use a car. That's straightforward, but it takes maybe two days to blast a way in. Then there is a day's journey to the centre. On balance, I would think we should use the sure way and make a planetfall in the twilight zone.'

Galloway said, 'There'll be no people, then, to object to all this?'

'No. Plantos died millennia ago. First they went underground in a series of interconnected cities. Then, it seems, they closed down one by one. Retreated to a last centre, under the darkside. Finally disappeared.'

Hulda put in an ethnological gloss. 'There is reference to the culture in some of the Cappodanian legends. The original inhabitants were of the same ethnic group and it is possible that ships from Plantos first colonized Cappodan. They believe that the people still live on.'

Simpson said, 'Any comment from those cherry lips is welcome, Commissar; but alive or dead they were no problem. I would agree with Commander Fletcher. One difficulty arises, however. I remember, Fletcher, that in your report, you described wall-to-wall seals that had to be blasted open. Are they still open? And, for that matter, are we sure we can find

71

the same radial? Following that, what equipment do we have? You and Cameron were using military scout cars with heavy calibre laser.'

It was a staff officer's contribution, which Fletcher felt he could have done without. He was spared direct answer by an intervention from the Fingalnan faction. Gimel-Sin said, 'Maps of the underground system were available to the navigation staff of *Leviathon*. I have a copy. I would say we should follow Commander Fletcher's advice. We can pick up the reference of the tunnel which he breached. Without stops to break the sealing bulkheads, it is a straightforward run to the centre. *Leviathon* went direct for the main city, but only a supership would have the power to cut into the rock and permafrost to make entry that way.'

Hulda was watching him closely and Fletcher got a relay of a view from a direct vision port which had him gripping the ward room table to steady his wheeling head.

He recognized the *locale* as a typical shot of the darkside of Plantos. Blue-black ice. Angular basalt, tilted every which-way and a familiar dune-like ridge which marked the surface projection of an underground city. It was bathed in brilliant light, a circular area, centred on the dune, which turned into instant lava like a lake of bubbling pitch.

The picture cut off and he was looking directly across the table to Hulda. Following the direction of her eyes, he turned to Gimel-Sin. There was no doubt about it, he had been aboard *Leviathon*. It was not surprising that no one had recognized him. There must have been ninety or more Fingalnans ferried out by the squadron. Added to which, they all looked alike. Small build, compact, silvery skin, oval faced and except for the very young and very old, virtually ageless.

He said, 'What rank did you hold on *Leviathon*, Number One? I should remember you, but I don't.' It was said in a tone that made no concessions to possible error.

For the first time, Gimel-Sin looked genuinely surprised.

72

He said, 'It no longer matters. I do not have any reason to conceal it. I was a staff adviser on navigation to Admiral Xantu. Do not think that I hold any personal grudge against you. We are professionals. One does not win every engagement.'

'But you did not need my help. You could have used any charter ship from any line and done your own navigating.'

'That is true, but your arrival was opportune and also as a well-known I.G.O. sympathizer your support made the mission less likely to outside interference.'

'I still think your government went the wrong way about it. A direct request to I.G.O. for the recovery of your property would have been given sympathetic hearing.'

'But too much publicity, Commander. That must have been explained to you. This could easily have become a scramble for treasure.'

Again Hulda intervened, but whatever reservation Gimel-Sin had, was firmly shoved below the transfer areas of his mind. All that came out, was a diffused impression of deliberate concealment, an impression that the sanctions behind it were very strong and were indeed bound up with survival. Veck or some other, had done a good job of motivation. The Fingalnan was set on a suicide course—to achieve an objective which was definitely not the one that appeared on the surface, or to die in the attempt. There would be no going back with an incomplete assignment.

It put a different complexion on the status of the civilian crew. Presumably, they too were expendable. Indeed, it seemed more than likely that if they got on to the true nature of the mission, they would not be allowed to get back and spread the news about.

What was left in the hulk to trigger off all the brou-ha-ha?

Aloud, Fletcher said, 'That settles it then.' He looked at his watch and the course duplicate in the wardroom roof. 'All stations call in thirty minutes. Two proving orbits and then planetfall. Bring your chart to the control cabin now

C*

Number One and I'll confirm the reference for the tunnel entrance. Any questions?'

Konstet was a silent ship. There was a quality about Plantos Three which inhibited speech. Europeans recognized it as an unexpected presentation, in real terms, of the Medieval concept of hell. Two hemispheres took each idea of satanic chaos to the ultimate. A region of cold with thick-ribbed ice, darkness and fantastic landscapes of black rock, succeeded a region of pitiless heat where the arid desert was baked in continuous eye-catching light.

They came down like a falling spear into the twilight zone. *Konstet* flexed majestically on her hydraulic jacks and added her own bizarre touch to a landscape empty of human artifacts.

In front, the horizon was an intense blue-black, pitted with brilliants. Behind them, a hot yellow dawn was permanently fixed like a painted line. Below the ship, under the straddled, tripod legs was black ice, in a shining pool that reflected the underbelly like a grotesque silver bowl.

Trudy Brogan cued in the robot sampler and a light sighing wind sounded from the tannoy. It carried a harmonic of cold and desolation, like the cry of a petrel. Gauges ran definitively into the red quadrants of sub-zero thermal agitation and oxygen deficiency.

Fletcher thought that, whatever there was of value on Plantos, it was not the planet itself. Anybody could have it.

Chapter Five

Any lingering doubt about the seriousness of Fingalnan
planning for the Plantos venture was nailed stone dead, when
Furvil and Lurdak—the second navigation detail—broke out
the excursion module and took it in a proving run round
the ship.

Fletcher had checked it as physically present, in its parking bay above the port rocket housing; but a number of
refinements were only apparent when it was seen in full, on
the main scanner. The Fingalnans had spent time and
imagination on it, working with knowledge of the terrain and
a clear idea of what they had to do.

It was hung about with ancillary gear like a tinker's mule.
Galloway said, 'Very cunnin', these wee silver bastards. All to
the good, though, Commander. I'll no be complainin' if it
shortens the time we hang about in this hole in hell.'

He was destined to take a closer look. Fletcher reckoned
that he needed the best engineer specialist he could get to sort
out the problems on the site. His memory of *Leviathon* was of
a shattered column of tangled wreckage. There would be no
walking in through a hatch and picking up the safe. The
Fingalnans were good, but weak on spontaneous improvisa-
tion.

Hard bargaining with Gimel-Sin produced a fairly balanced
crew for the scout car. Fletcher, Galloway, and Hulda, by
her own request, on the I.G.O. side were joined by Gimel-Sin,
Furvil and Lurdak.

Simpson, with Bramah, Fergus and Trudy Brogan had the
remaining seven Fingalnans to watch. As the excusion party
filed into the car port, Fletcher recognized that the base con-
tingent could well have the harder time of it. If there was

treachery intended, the push would come when they returned with the jackpot. Survival would depend on getting on board.

He held back and spoke to Simpson in the reception bay. Monitored or not, it had to be said. 'I know you'll have thought of it; but there just could be a take-over intended. Once we go underground, there's radio screening. You can't reach us. Keep our people together and stay on watch.'

'That's so. Don't worry about this end. Look out for squalls yourself when you find the strong box.'

'Why do you say that?'

'Let's say, I have a hunch about it.'

On the ground, Fletcher was faced with a question mark of his own. Two kilometres off from *Konstet* and she was a shadowy spar in a desolation that bit down into the mind. Now he remembered it, and he could not believe that he had given it enough weight in Veck's office. Surely, he should have known that he was taking on a very dodgy mission?

Last time, there had been support from a full squadron with a command post on *Europa* calling the shots. Now he had a small, divided force with no reserves. Any breakdown in the car would not just be an inconvenience, it could be fatal.

His voice had a new, astringent harmonic when he called the course readings to Furvil.

Light levels zeroed and the dawn band dropped below the horizon. A searchlight probe like a white lance thrust ahead with its tip breaking in a bright asterisk on smooth, black ice.

The car raced with a sonar beam bouncing ahead, feeling a path over spurs and pillars of rock that appeared without any logic out of the permafrost floor.

In thirty minutes, they were well into a world that not only did not live, but could not imaginably have lived since the beginning. Sentient man had no place there; thinking man was only proving that he did not think to any purpose in allowing himself to be conned into going there.

For the first time, when physically close to Hulda, Fletcher picked up no subtle radiation from that beacon psyche. Sheer pressure from a totally brutal environment had bludgeoned every delicate mental feeler into a state of numb shock.

Surprisingly, he found her more interesting. A person he could get near. She was reduced to the level of being a run-of-the-mill honey, wanting reassurance from an expert, that all manner of things would be well in the long term. Visor hinged back in the controlled atmosphere of the car, she looked at him with wide grey eyes, innocent of all knowledge of what was going on in his head.

The fact that, in spite of the unfolding panorama, his computer was clocking up lechery, was another proof that she was out of phase on the E.S.P. level.

She said, 'I didn't want to stay on the ship with your jokey friend Simpson, but this is a horrible place.'

Had she been receiving strength nine, she might have complained that the commentary in Fletcher's head was no better than the Commodore's and that she might just as well have been propositioned in comfort. In effect, now that she was not looking through the surface appearance to what went on in his head, she, also, saw him better as a person and took a few seconds in a direct stare to register it, as though seeing him for the first time.

Packed together on the middle seat of the six-seater car, their heads were near enough for a telepathic bonanza; but Fletcher was only conscious of a very feminine ambience, as though uncorked from a bottle by the tipping away of her dome seal. A scent of assent, with a sense of strain in the narrow dielectric between them.

The electric disturbance was purely sensual and when she belatedly recognized that admiration was rearing its ugly head, she was relying on the same visual clues as any other girl in a similar situation.

A lean brown face was turned her way, with the left eye-brow given a piratical slant by the pucker of a radiation burn. Near enough to touch with a stretched tongue. Now,

77

for a change, she was at the receiving end of a kind of invasion of privacy.

Dag Fletcher recognized her problem and moved the conversation to a National Geographic level with philosophic overtones. 'What I don't understand is why there are no recognizable architectural remains on the surface. Not even on the light side. At one time, they must have been surface dwellers. It's an empty canvas; however, it is said that the highest pleasure does not rest in passive watching of nature's diversity, but in what the mind itself is looking for and finds by forcing its own pattern on what it sees.'

Even with E.S.P. in eclipse, she judged nobody talked that way without using words as a cover for unseasonable thought. She reacted in a more normal fashion with a flash of old-style pique. 'You are treating me as a child, Commander. I know there is no serious danger; but I hate the thought of perpetual cold and darkness. Also, I think of the people who lived here and knew what was coming. It must have made a degrading change in the *quality* of life.'

'As far as I could judge, there was no disorder. The rooms in the houses in the cities were swept clean and sealed. Murals are of a happy people. Much like the pictures of Knossos on Earth planet. Very sympathetic. Dark-haired types like your own culture on Bromius.'

He stopped short and she looked closely at him. Something there had triggered off a sequence in the holographic web of memory.

Interest had relaxed her tensions and she was able to share the experience in a partial way. The chief element in the recall was a long frieze, seen from a point ten metres distant and through a transparent screen. A circular torch beam was scanning along its length, highlighting aspects of a market scene. Vivid, but unfamiliar, fruits, a silvery fish with triangular scales, individuals and groups appearing in the moving circle and having the illusion of life. Then the torch steadied and settled for a dark girl, who was surely alive,

78

head back and turned to look straight out of the picture at the viewing eye.

Fletcher's reacting affective tone sent a surge to the delicate galvanometer in her head. It had made a big impact on him at that time and even the memory of it could move him again. In words, she got the gloss, 'Whoever painted her was in love with his model. This flat copy has more life than most women in 3-D flesh.'

There was a half second more to look at the freize, as though it was projected on the hurrying, black wall outside the car and she felt that she was on the verge of penetrating some second veil to a different reality behind the image, when Mark Twain Furvil called sharply, 'Objective, dead ahead, Excellency.'

The picture collapsed. Fletcher's mood changed to a grim recognition that his co-pilot was a bigger fish than had so far been admitted. It raised the whole question of how straight Veck had been about the project. There had to be something else behind it and Simpson's arrival was no accident.

Resolution of that problem would have to wait. Not long now, anyway before the Fingalnans would have to show their hand.

The objective was a long tumulus, running away out of the limits of vision. It was ten metres broad on its flat top, rising maybe four metres high, by short steep ramps. Time had not yet erased the traces of human activity on the site. Blurred, oblong depressions showed where cars had rested and dug themselves protective pits. As Furvil took them in a tight turn, across the hump, they could see a deep shaft sunk into the permafrost.

There was no lock in the small car. One out, all out. Fletcher said, 'Come down midway across the excavation. Keep power on and lift a few centimetres every five minutes. Otherwise, she'll freeze solid and need a heat line to dig her out. Seal up all hands. As soon as we get down, I'm going out.'

The skids straddled the width, with a half metre's purchase

at either side. Furvil equalized pressure and slid the plexidome forward. Communication was by mime or by one-to-one contact on a wandering lead from the miniature console on the chest of each suit.

Through two visors, Hulda was as remote as a fish in another aquarium. Rational fear had beaten her back again to the perimeter of her own head. She was looking at the gauges on her left arm as though she would have been better pleased not to know, but forced by morbid curiosity to see the worst.

Head and shoulders through the hatch, with his feet feeling for the rungs of a flexible ladder that dropped into the pit, Dag Fletcher leaned across and plugged himself into her pianola.

Her eyes were very wide, with dilated pupils and he had to point to her head before she switched in the circuit that made her okay for sound.

In a moment of insight, he picked up something of the problem she must have, with the difficult missions that came her way as an I.G.O. Commissar. Come to that, it was an amazing thing that she had reached the grade at all. Bromius culture was a particularly delicate flower and its people were less tough-minded than any in the galaxy. Refined aesthetics were their meat. But then, as a blonde, she would be regarded as a freak. That would have a conditioning effect in itself. Every human being was motivated to try to think well of itself. Compensation factors would come into it. She had driven herself hard to get where she was and, in some situations, there was still a basic insecurity that was hard to buck.

He said, 'Never take reality at face value. And speaking of face values, you have an oil slick on your left cheek bone that gives you an appealing apache look. Keep an eye on His Excellency, until I get back.'

He whipped out the jack and disappeared, before she could reply; but it was a nicely calculated intrusion, that did nothing but good. A bit to stimulate thought, a bit to stir up the self-regarding instinct and a small useful task.

It was as well that he missed the reply, though she spoke it out for her own comfort to the inside of her shell, 'When I need psychotherapy from a half-educated *barbarian,* I'll ask for it.'

Indignation took her mind off the gauges. Then she realized that it had done that thing and wondered whether indeed he had meant it to work in that way. How subtle was he, at that?

Hulda broke out the seat clips and heaved herself through the hatch to stand on the roof. Down below, Fletcher was digging about with a vibrator probe.

She forced herself to look around the set. Straight ahead, the searchlight beamed out along the whole back of the ridge. Left and right, darkness was that much more absolute. Moving a centimetre at a time, she shuffled round a hundred and eighty degrees to look back from where they had come. Now her eyes adjusted to the darkness and she could see colour in the round stars, unrefracted by an atmosphere. 'Never take reality at face value'—what was anybody supposed to make of that? At worst it was meaningless, at best it was trite.

Reality was there present and had to be reckoned with on its own terms. A lot of it at that. More than a finite mind could take in. Even in this desolate wilderness.

A small silver asterisk separated itself from a star cluster and crossed into an area where it was lost again in a depth pattern of unimaginable numbers. She was moving to complete the circle and get back inside, when it caught her eye again, as though she had triggered it off by moving her head.

Forgetting caution, she took a full step towards the hatch and was caught out by low gravity. To any frozen observer, it would have appeared that she made a clumsy hop and dived head first into the pit.

Panic flashed out an indiscriminate, psychokinetic surge and alerted Fletcher to look up. The spotlight in his visor picked up the human plummet which was as unexpected in its way as any shooting star.

Like Lorna Diment, when surprised by her rodent, Hulda jerked out a Bromusian variant of 'Eek', which was still echoing inside her helmet, when free fall ended with her head half a centimetre from the deck.

Even with low gravity, catching her had been a physical *tour-de-force,* and Fletcher found his eyes filled with sweat, which beat the recirculating system for a count of five. Simultaneously, his mind was flooded by a warm, pink glow of thanks.

When both cleared he found that Hulda had taken her weight on her hands and he was looking through the open V of her waving legs to the black wall of the vault.

A couplet ran in his head, 'The grave's a fine and private place. But none, I think, do there embrace.'

The pink glow was succeeded by a small spasm of diffused colours which might be regarded as a psychic blush and he had to concede that the commissar was at a disadvantage. Shifting his grip to the crotch and a tethering cleat in the gorgette, he set her round on her feet and plugged his wandering lead into the jack on her console.

'What's this, then? Dropping in for a chat?'

Although her English was good, she missed the small joke and answered seriously, emotion shifting her vocal range by a richer semitone of depth. 'I thought you should know, there's a bright speck moving overhead. It could be another ship.'

Fletcher thought bitterly, 'That figures. That's all I need. I should have told Veck to get himself knotted. Too many people know all about it. Whichever way it goes, the Fingalnan agency will be under suspicion. If it's a Scotian in a parking orbit we're set up for destruction. On the other hand, he might not have found us yet. It will take days to run an exhaustive surface scan to isolate a ship. Might just as well recover this package and see what it's all about.'

Aloud he said, 'Do they know about it upstairs?'

'I don't think so. I was the only one outside.'

'Then we'd better get on and finish this exercise. Are you okay?'

'Thank you. Yes.'

'Up you go then. Don't mention what you saw. Tell Gimel-Sin to lower a heat line and the grab. Two pulls on the cable and I want a slow, steady lift. We cut a section under here to take a car, with a lock behind it to conserve pressure. There was breathable air in the tunnel system.'

When she had gone, he worked at the centre of the site with the hand vibrator. The tunnel roof had been left clear, but now there was a covering of ice almost ten centimetres deep. By the time the thin hose snaked down beside him, he had uncovered two undercut cleats, which had been fashioned out of the metre-thick roof to take lifting hawsers.

Fletcher stood clear and let the grab fall, then he made fast and took up the slack on its ratchet until there was only enough play to allow Furvil to make his frost-beating moves.

Trailing the heat line like an umbilical cord, he started at one corner and sprayed round the perimeter of the oblong area.

Watching through a viewing port in the floor of the car, Hulda saw him disappear in a boiling cloud of white vapour.

Following instructions to the letter, Furvil lifted the car fractionally and settled it back. On the small scanner, Fletcher's bulky shape appeared briefly, wreathed in mist.

Lurdak at the winch, and hooked up to the console, called 'Signal to lift.'

The car vibrated as though it would shake every last rivet out of its seat. Downdraught swept the hole clear and the scanner showed a foreshortened view of the trog, standing on the slab, close to the hawser and looking up.

Hulda could just make out the line of his face set back behind the pressure helmet and picked up a gloss that showed he had recognized her. It was set to a rhythm which must have been an Earth type tune she had not heard, 'Who's

83

that up there, saying who's that down here? Who's that?'

The man had no sense of the danger he was in. If the cable broke, he could be cut in strips.

Down below, Fletcher got a diffused newsflash that she wished him well and waved a gauntlet at the underbelly of the car. Under his feet, he felt the slab lurch. Through his gauntlet, he could feel the cable going thin under strain. He had never known one to break. In theory the car motor should cut out with a safety margin before that could happen but the same thought crossed his mind that had occurred already to Hulda with a lot more force.

Furvil was juggling delicately to offset the thin ghost of a wind that was trying to shift the car out of a vertical rise. He could see that if the clumsy slab touched anywhere along its length, they would slew round and jam into the sides.

There was silence in the car, except for the frenetic whine of the overloaded power pack and even Galloway had to concede that the man was doing a good job. A centimetre at a time, the plate crawled up the shaft with shards of ice dropping into the narrow freeway at its edges.

A half metre from the lip and a jagged, metre-square wedge upended itself and plugged the gap. The slab began to tilt and then ground a sharp corner into the wall of permafrost.

Furvil slammed into the red quadrant for emergency power and the car bucked as if kicked up the tail.

The motor sent up a banshee howl and the slab was plucked free like a cork coming out of a bottle. Caught by the wind, it swayed wildly and Furvil released the grab.

It was a nicely-calculated move. With the momentum of its swing, it would be pitched clear of the hole. The fact that Fletcher was standing on it was a secondary matter. They had arrived. He was expendable.

Hulda got onto it, a nonasecond before he pushed the lever to jettison. A confused hunch of what could happen reached the human pendulum as Furvil's hand moved.

Without waiting to think it through, Fletcher snapped the

toggle of his friction line on to the bottom rung of the ladder and felt the floor slip away from under his feet.

Free from its anchoring weight, the car went up to its maximum ceiling like a free standing elevator, with Fletcher going down, spider fashion, as the tether paid out.

Three metres from the ground, he thumped the release and took the drop on his foam-filled boots in a sliding stop that sent him fifty metres along the top of the ridge.

There was no doubt about the intention behind the move. The car wheeled against the black backdrop like an illuminated slug. It occurred to Fletcher that what Furvil or Gimel-Sin had done was too obvious to explain away. If they knew it had failed, there was nothing to stop them finishing it once and for all with a burst of laser fire from the heavy gauge tube under the skids. He switched out his visor light and began a shambling run back to the hole.

It opened up at his feet, before he realized it was near and he had to throw himself back to save himself from a fall that would have done a neat job of destruction for them.

The car was coming back. Acceleration in low gravity had taken Furvil three kilometres from the site. Now the white beam of its searchlight was racing over the ground.

Fletcher swivelled round, got his hands on the rim and went down to a full arm stretch. The ledge left by the slab was hardly more than twenty centimetres, but if he dropped true it would break his fall. Below that, the floor of the tunnel was another twelve metres down. Even in low gravity, it was on the threshold of tolerance for the impact absorption factors of the suit.

The penumbra ahead of the advancing light was thinning out as he let go. His feet hit the ledge and slipped back, then he was in free fall again with hardly a check. Down into pitch darkness, his mind counting out the distance, so that there was a small intellectual satisfaction in hitting the floor at precisely the expected second.

As he struck, he bent the bulky suit for a forward roll and

felt himself tumbling like any padded clown on an ankle deep carpet of fine dust. When he stopped, he had no idea which way was up or down. He was reduced to a mind without orientation. I think therefore I am. But what am I?

Anger was a thread through the maze. With Othello, he felt he could say, 'I am not valiant neither, that every puny whipster gets my sword.' From Veck to Furvil, the Fingalnans had done what they liked with him.

On hands and knees, he waited for a count of five with his eyes closed. Then he got to his feet and looked up.

He had rolled clear of the gap in the roof and could see it now marked out as a smoky pallor on the darkness as the car manoeuvred overhead for a clean drop.

If they looked closely they would see the swirling dust and know he was there. On the other hand, the downdraught would in any case make a sandstorm of it. They would have to wait until it settled before they could locate the lock.

Light was coming down in a solid shaft when he picked out the bulkhead that Cameron's crew had improvized to hold the atmosphere in the complex. He had reached it and set himself against it between two heavy release wheels, when the turbulence from the car's motors ripped down and lifted the dust in a solid cloud.

From a black void he was plunged in a white void and he reckoned there was nothing to choose. It could have been a bag dropped over his visor. Working by touch alone, he took time to unclip his laser from its pouch on his left leg and uncoiled its lanyard before he lifted it out. If it dropped, there would be no finding it again. When the loop was around his neck, he brought it out and shifted its selector for a wide-angle stunning beam. Not that he could find any rational objection to killing Furvil; but if there was only time for one shot he wanted to stop them all.

Now the mist was intensely bright, but he still could not see his hand when he brought it up in front of his visor. Not even the direct beam of the headlight would pick him out.

Vibration stopped. The car had settled on its skids. They would wait now for the mist to clear. By coming straight in without stopping to see if he had survived the fall, they had made a plain statement of attitude. The first yet.

It had not gone without protest from the rest of the crew. Hulda had done her best to send out a warning, but had no idea whether it had been received. She could sense the mood behind Furvil's action and knew that he believed Fletcher would not survive the drop.

As the load had come off and the car accelerated away, Furvil closed the hatch and air pressure automatically adjusted. Her voice fairly crackled out of the external speaker and she used Fingalnan to make sure there was no language barrier. 'Why did you do that? You must go down and pick up the Commander.'

Galloway was struggling out of his seat harness to get at the console and take over.

It was left to Lurdak in the small freight bay, where the winch gear was housed, to stabilize the situation. He said simply, 'Shall I kill them now, Excellency?'

Gaelic common-sense stopped Galloway in his tracks. He would be no help dead. He dropped back into his seat.

Gimel-Sin said, 'There is likely to be an enquiry. It will be best if they suffer equipment failure. Wait. Unless of course, they make any threatening move.'

Working behind the words of his mental set, Hulda knew it was no bluff. She said, 'This is not an intelligent action. Any gain that comes of it will be temporary and local. You will never get back in the ship without us. You under-rate Commodore Simpson if you believe he will accept any explanation of selective accidents.'

It was heard and made its point, but there was no reply. Furvil was trimming the car to lie fore and aft on the long axis of the excavation. Gimel-Sin was searching the area with the scanner. Lurdak was simply watchful with a heavy service laser trained midway and ready to swing on any necessary target.

There was no sign of Fletcher. The grey rectangular trepan had rolled end-over-end on impact and was off the top of the barrow. Failing anywhere else, it looked as though a happy quirk of mechanical forces had put him under it. That was accident number one, arranged as neatly as any assassin could contrive.

Certainly, it seemed to give the Admiral every satisfaction. He left the search and homed on the pit. A white cloud was boiling slowly out of it. But there was no problem yet in locating the entrance. Furvil judged it to a centimetre and went down in a copy-book manoeuvre equidistant from every side.

Light was refracted to its source. A white glare covered the plexidome and every viewing port. The sonar probe found the floor and brought them down with a feather touch that hardly shoved in the dampers on suspension.

Any place was a better place to be than the surface of Plantos. But except for a sense of re-entry into the womb, there was no immediate gain. Gimel-Sin got round to answering Hulda's query, which had hung about long enough to go stale.

'There is something in what you say. When I have satisfied myself that you are unarmed, Lurdak can put his laser away. The property we are collecting is extremely valuable. I was not sure that Commander Fletcher intended to honour his agreement. As to you. We shall see. Do nothing rash and all might yet be well for you.'

A clear, dark circle appeared at the top of the plexidome and expanded slowly, giving the impression that the car itself was floating to the surface of a sea of milk. Furvil shot back the hatch and a trickle of fine dust dropped into the car.

Gimel-Sin motioned for them to bale out. Although he was satisfied that they were unarmed, he wanted them in front of the column.

Now, the car's lights were making sense of the space. They were within the arched span of a flattened half-cylinder. Twelve metres to the hole that had given them entrance; a width of twenty-five metres from edge to edge of the roadway; long axis twenty metres to the rear; closed, ten metres ahead of the car, by a metallic bulkhead.

Still crotch deep, or more, according to length of leg, in milk soup, the column trecked over to the lock. Fletcher had moved to a point behind the car and rose silently to his feet to become the tail-end Charlie of the caravan.

It was clowning of a kind, which gave him a certain savage pleasure. First of all, he shot Lurdak and caught him as he fell, lowering him below smog level.

In theory, he could have worked his way to the front, and had in fact reached a point where he could tap Gimel-Sin on his shoulder, when Hulda picked up his radiation.

He felt her incredulous surge of hope and unaffected pleasure in his survival. Then she turned to see if it was a true thing. Gimel-Sin reacted nervously and followed her round. The movement of his feet being shrouded, he appeared to twist from the waist like a sectional puppet.

Expecting Lurdak, what he saw was all bad news and he made every effort to grab the laser that was hanging by a short lanyard from his right wrist.

Fletcher had taken first pressure when he had second thoughts. From all the evidence, Gimel-Sin was the only one on the set who had been briefed to find the safe and knew precisely what it was they were looking for. Putting him in cold storage for forty-eight hours would be no big help. He was near enough to drop his own laser to swing on its lanyard and grab for the moving wrist.

When Furvil looked back from the lock door to signal that he had it all buttoned up and they could move in, he was faced by a semicircle of spectators. Galloway had the admiral's laser. Fletcher had recovered his own. Hulda and

Gimel-Sin were neutral observers.

He fell forward with surprise clamped on his face like any mask. Hulda transmitted a high-voltage mixture of shock and reproach, thinking that he was dead. It was followed by a rationalizing bit, as she conceded that Fletcher had a case.

When they were in the car and pressure made speech possible, she was glad to find that judgement had, anyway, been premature.

Working the controls himself Fletcher moved them into the lock. He said to Gimel-sin, 'I don't follow your reasoning, but believe this, if you try anything else, you won't survive it. Nor will the two we leave here. From now on in, just concentrate on picking up the parcel and getting back to *Konstet.*'

When the far door opened, he drove slowly into the first tunnelway and stopped to take stock. Memory of it flooded his mind. As before, there was subdued light from what remained of self-energizing units, set in oval ceiling ports. Walls stretched away like an exercise in perspective to an indefinite distance. But there was one factor that did not jell and he was half a minute sorting it out. Except for the spirals of dust which they had brought through with them, the roadway was grey and gleaming as though it had been freshly metalled.

Chapter Six

Impressions were crowding Fletcher. Overlapping his own recall was a diffused sense of being under threat, which he tracked down to Hulda as soon as Galloway reported that there was breathable air outside the car.

She shoved back her visor and unmasked a face innocent of all colour. Fletcher asked, 'What is it? I thought you would be the first to approve of a man-made system and a light to see by.'

For the first time, she had no positive answer, 'I don't know. I can only say that there is a powerful, psychokinetic field. Antipathetic to us. We are not welcome here. Don't you feel it?'

'Not on my account. Maybe it's a hangover from the last tenants. But they're long gone. I can tell you the place is a museum. There was no trace of life. You'll see as we go through.'

'Please make it as quick as you can. I tell you, seriously, this is worse than the surface.'

Fletcher moved the car forward on zero thrust for a hundred metres and set it down again.

Gimel-Sin asked sharply, 'Why have you stopped?'

'Every so far, the roadway has a section that pivots. Acts as a trap. Just ahead is the first one we hit. Half way over and your weight takes it down, drops you in a pit and swings back to fix you inside. My group bought it and we had a long job cutting out.'

'But this does not matter in a car. We can cross before the mechanism operates.'

'Quite so. But one of my men was killed by the fall. We left him there. I want to see if he is still all right.'

Hulda had broken out the seals on her suit and peeled it off. She was filling a borrowed lime-green coverall to its brim, and had unleased a spectacular bell of pale hair from its chiffon tether. Even this personal therapy had not set her mind at rest. She said, 'Why? What can have happened to him? The dead are dead. Whether "all right" or not is a matter for argument. But what good can it do to look?'

There was something in what she said. But Fletcher was remembering Geratty. Making a call on the man's family had been one of the worst chores of his early career. In an obscure way, he felt he owed it to them to visit the vault.

He also remembered the dust and resealed his visor which was a useful gesture for ending any debate. His voice came thinly from the external speaker. 'I'm moving the car to straddle this edge. That will hold it while I cross to where we made a hole. Don't shift it any farther or the car itself will go in.'

When it was done, he climbed out. They saw him clip a safety line to the leading skid and walked ahead. Three paces out and there was a stir of movement as the roadway tried to turn.

Ten metres ahead, he veered right and knelt down at a small, circular patch of discolouration. Working with a hand vibrator, he cleared round the site and dug out a covering plate.

Fletcher could feel the mounting tension in Hulda's mind. It was getting to be a nuisance. He was altogether too suggestible. She should have stayed in the ship. After all, she was a big girl and used to defending her corner. He should have left her to take her chance with Simpson. For that matter, the man was no fool. He would know better than to push too hard on an I.G.O. official. This way, he was liable to lose his own judgement in any dicey situation that came up.

With the plate clear, he went down prone and wriggled head and shoulders through the gap, like any patient eskimo at a seal hole. Light from his dome dropped in a white column and he checked out the floor along the far wall. That was where they had left their Elpenor with his shattered nape nerve. He had been stretched out in the centre, arms folded across his chest, on a dune of white dust like a catafalque.

Nothing came up on the first traverse, not even a carpet of dust. The ribbed floor of porcelain tile was clear to see. Fletcher thought irritably, 'It's that damned girl in my head, orientation's gone to hell. I'm looking along the wrong side.'

A small flare of anger pushed her away and he went round on a methodical pattern of search. Then he heaved himself out and boosted output to call across to the car. 'Galloway. An inspection lamp.'

Hulda brought it across, stepping delicately on the sprung roadway. He lowered it into the hole and took another look. There was no longer any doubt. The plain rectangular box was empty. SM 3695 Geratty K.V. late of the corvette *Petrel*, had slipped anchor for the second time.

Fletcher shoved back the plate and sat still to think it out, automatically going through the motions of unsealing his pressure helmet. Hulda asked, 'What is it?' and was ignored.

Finally, he had it straight. Garatty had not been moved by the squadron. The ships had been overfull, ferrying the many survivors from *Leviathon*. The question of taking Geratty or any of the other dead crewmen back for burial had never come up. It would not have been on.

Waiting patiently for the *guru* to come out of his trance, Hulda went into a full knee bend and squatted back on her heels. It brought them to a common eye level and she could see that Fletcher was not seeing her at all. She tried again, 'What is it?'

This time, his mind shifted from its problem and found another. The taut pose she was in presented as complete an antithesis to any idea of death as an allegorist could find. He had not wanted her on the trip as an official. Now he recognized a personal angle. She was a threat to his peace of mind. Not only from the disturbing E.S.P. point of view, but as an individual. He did not want her harmed.

Accompanying the verbal text of thought, there was a running animated strip in full colour, which took the personal interest to a hypothetical climax, with Hulda in the elegant Bromusian national dress that left the heart bare, walking towards him with arms open in welcome.

Before he could speak, she had jumped to her feet and turned her back. He caught her as she reached the car and stopped her climbing through the hatch by penning her against the side. 'I'm sorry about that. You've only yourself to blame. You shouldn't read my mind. Or if you do, you should take the rough with the smooth.'

Appeasement got him nowhere. She said, 'Don't apologize, Commander. I am only surprised that you have no serious notion of the danger we are in. I have long been convinced that the Earth ethnic type is basically frivolous. It amazes me that you have survived as long as you have. In this instance, I am more concerned, because my own survival is dependent on your efficiency. Also this mission has a wider importance than you know. Please concentrate on what we have to do and get back to the ship. Let me go.'

Fletcher pitched his helmet into the car and used his free hand to turn her round. Back to the curved shell plate, the strain on the borrowed fabric was hitting an interesting crisis threshold. Beauty and the beast at that. Her eyes flickered an acknowledgment that she had appreciated the gloss and was all in favour of the beast bit of the equation.

He said, 'Hulda, I can't entirely control what I think and you must know the impact you make. But I can tell you it won't alter my purpose. I didn't ask you along. I'd rather you were not here. But you are and we both have to do the best we can with the situation. Okay?'

With one kilometre on the clock, Fletcher stopped the car again. This time there was no question. A solid silver-grey bulkhead filled the tunnel from edge to edge.

Gimel-Sin showed that the Fingalnans had done some checking round the complex while *Leviathon* was in hiding. He said, 'These screens are put in at all the entry points to the cities. Operating mechanism is sited, as you would expect, on the inside. You will have to cut a way for a man to go through and work the gear.'

'Not this time,' Dag Fletcher was already on the way out, 'We worked along this section on foot. There is a hole we can use.'

He was, however, some time finding the site of the break. They saw him running his hands over the surface and making trial cuts into the ceramic facing before he hit the right panel and could prise out the seal.

When he disappeared through the hole there was a stage wait that lengthened to a long five minutes before the barrier began to move.

While it was in position, it was a convenient blank screen for projecting whatever the three watchers had in mind. For Galloway, it was a drawing board which he filled with a variety of possible operating mechanisms for the lifting gear that could be used to move it. Gimel-Sin was remembering the last sight he had of *Leviathon,* before an I.G.O. car had taken him out in the general surrender. She had fallen across a wide piazza with the entry hatches to the ground. Unless there were breaks in the fabric, there would be no easy way through. Also, the I.G.O. demolition team had stayed behind to disarm the hulk. It would depend on what they had done.

Hulda, out of all season, was looking at a numinous picture of an ancient tomb. Something she had not seen in the flesh, but which had come, by a quirk of free association, out of a school history tape, on ancient cultures of other worlds. Even the title was there in Prisma type face like an exercise in Op Art.

It was the Taj Mahal, a pale, marble artifact, that had always appealed to the Bromusians as a harmonious state-ment of an attitude of mind similar to their own.

Its reflection, in a still pool, seemed as solid and habitable as the original. She saw herself diving into the water and entering the building, as though it was a rational thing and only an idiot would take the surface manifestation as the important aspect of the double image.

Then the screen had silently lifted into the roof and she was looking along the roadway, past Fletcher to a huge natural cavern, brilliantly lit by roof ports arranged in concentric circles round a centre sun.

There was no comment as Fletcher moved the car on. The roadway was carried forward on a flyover, set on slim, cantilevered pylons and made out at the far side into another tunnel mouth which did not appear to be blocked.

In the centre, branch roads curved symmetrically left and right in a clover leaf to carry vehicles down to floor level.

For the first time, there was a lavish use of colour, subtle and harmonious. Tall building blocks had balanced areas of pale, pastel shades that gave space and warmth as though the set were glowing with natural light.

Even Gimel-Sin made no overt objection, when Fletcher left the main artery and planed into the square.

He set the car down on an area of amethyst tile bounded by formal gardens. The air was heavy with the scent of verbena. At ground level, the city seemed huge and shimmering as though every perspective was infinite.

Hulda said, 'It would be possible to live here without missing the outside. They were very advanced in environmental engineering.'

'Were?' Galloway, as a practical man had walked over to pluck a flower, 'I only know that growth like this needs regular care. I'd say they're still at it. Was it like this, Commander, when you were here before?'

The answer came from Gimel-Sin. 'What has happened here, Commander? Did you know of this? For what purpose did your organization go to this length of reconstruction?'

'I did not know of it. As far as I know there has been no

visit to Plantos by an I.G.O. force since the *Leviathon* affair. We pulled out within days of the surrender, as you will remember. I don't understand what has happened.'

Speaking almost to himself, Gimel-Sin said, 'If not I.G.O. then who? Not the home planet of Cappodan. I would have heard about that. Who then? Who could have an interest in this remote place? It has long been established that there are no useful minerals on Plantos.'

Hulda moved away from the group and crossed a strip of blue grass to the paved forecourt of a tall apartment block.

She was a natural in the setting, stylish, as the people who had once walked about in the square. Fletcher saw her walk straight ahead, across the porch and into a recessed entrance hall. That was another thing. Memory stopped admiration of her long-legged elegance in its tracks. That should have been impossible. The houses had been mothballed in transparent plastic. The one she had entered without hindrance was indeed the one where he had first seen the long frieze behind its protective wall.

Dag Fletcher ran to catch up. As he did, he knew that there were at least two motives. One was to see that she came to no harm; but equally strong was the pull of the frieze itself. This time, he could get in close and take a detailed look at the picture of the dark girl. It was almost as though he had been told that he could meet her in the flesh.

Hulda was standing in the centre of the lobby turning slowly to check out the walls. She said without apology, 'If this is where your mural was, I don't see it now. Could you have made a mistake?'

'No it was here. Along the facing wall. A two-metre high strip running the full width.'

He ran his hands over the surface. Close to, it had a granulated texture, warm to the touch. There was still a strip of triangular beading to mark out a panel. Systematically he went along its length, pressing and twisting every few centimetres.

97

'Why do you do that?'

'Last time, we found doors operated by recessed tiles.'

When he found it, it was as though he had drawn a curtain from the window of a busy room. A thin, flexible covering sheet whipped smartly up like an opening eyelid and he was face to face with an image that had been part of the bric-a-brac of his mind for the intervening years.

Seen close, she was life size, as though sharing the same strip of parquet and all set to give his left ear a delighted bite. Honey-brown skin, glowed with positive health like an ad-man's gift for a wheat extract promotion. Kohl-rimmed eyes had the texture of black milk. She was an ecstatic, caught in mid-dance, nearest by Earth standards to a Gupta on an ancient Hindu temple. One for whom the act of love would be service to an idea of god.

For Hulda, seeing the tableau whole, and not susceptible to female erotics, it was further proof that there was something rotten in the state. She said, 'So you have found it. I recognize her. She is the girl you have had in your head. It would be better to have her exorcized. Can't you see that the culture it represents is alien to you? The whole scene is hysterical. It represents not happiness, which is rational, but frenzy which is destructive.'

It was a fair analysis. Although Fletcher could not see beyond his apsara there was a difference which he would have recognized in the tableau. What he had seen as the innocence of a golden age was now decadent, vicious even, turned in on itself, in a circular pursuit of sensation for its own sake.

If Fletcher heard, he gave no sign. She said, 'Commander,' and followed with, 'Commander Fletcher. Do you hear me?'

It was plain that he did not, and she tried to get through at an E.S.P. level. This time, there was no joy. He was on a closed circuit loop which left no opening for penetration. She was reminded of the Bromusian proverb—a drunkard, an idiot, a hungry man, a frightened man, a greedy man, a hasty man and a man in love will never do the right thing. It was no comfort.

Hulda had a moment's panic and then pushed past the zombie to reach up and twist the beading to reactivate the shutter. When it whipped into place, Fletcher shook his head like a baffled hound dog.

'Why did you do that?'

She was saved any reply by the arrival of Gimel-Sin and reckoned that whatever reason she had given would have been misunderstood.

The Fingalnan said, 'Commander, I don't like it. We should press on without further delay. If you are right and this is not the work of your people, we must be prepared for opposition.'

Fletcher said, 'Very well,' and walked past them both to the car without a backward look.

Finding allies where she could, Hulda hung back long enough to say to Gimel-Sin, 'I am sure you are right. Also, this place has some particular danger for Commander Fletcher. We must prevent him from becoming involved with these people.'

'Involved with what people, Commissar?'—Galloway, still holding his flower, had picked up the end of the transmission, 'You'll not be saying you've seen them?'

'Their influence is strong. In some sense they are still alive.'

To date, the mission had been no paradise for a conversationalist; the next leg would have made a holiday in the heart for a Trappist. Fletcher hunched himself over the controls and was out of reach of Hulda's probing mind. She gave up and sat back. Speed reached a ceiling at forty kilometres an hour, when the sonar probe automatically cut back power to keep the hurrying car within a safety margin, having regard to a series of convoluted curves like a demented gut.

White, blank walls went past as though the car was

stationary and a plain, tubular cloth was being whipped past its viewing ports. Time had no meaning. It could have been a day, or a week, before another bulkhead showed up and Fletcher put them down.

In fact, Hulda saw from the time disk that they were half an hour older and had notched up twenty kilometres of distance run.

The mechanical chore seemed to have cleared Fletcher's head. On the way through the hatch, he broke his silence with the first estimate of distances so far given. '*Leviathon* is in the fourth city on this radial. This is number two. About eighty kilometres on to number three. Then a short leg of about fifteen. With luck, not more than three hours. Say when you'd like a break.'

Since this last seemed to be levelled at herself, Hulda answered for the party, 'No breaks. Let's get there and get out.'

It earned her a brief, considering look, as though she did not appreciate her good fortune in being on such a safari.

When the curtain went up, they could have made a devious circuit and got back to the town they had left. It was another turn of the screw, another factor to reinforce the off-beat character of the enterprise.

If she had been asleep, Hulda would have been sure that Fletcher had made a detour and brought them round for a second run through. It undermined rational thought.

He saw the question in their eyes before anybody framed it. 'They follow a pattern. I guess they refined it so far, that they hit the ultimate in efficiency, so why deviate? You can't have too much of a perfect thing.'

That was in the same category of dark sayings as Rousseau's —'The majority may be wrong, nevertheless it is always right'; but Hulda let it pass unchallenged. This time, he crossed the flyover without a stop and plunged them into the ongoing tunnel at full speed.

A half hour stint had been bad. Two hours broke the

barriers of sense. Its only interest was in watching an impressive feat of concentration and expertise. Fletcher never faltered, never slackened speed. Sitting relaxed on the pilot chair, he held the car with mathematical accuracy on the centre of the half tube and drove as if it was running on a monorail.

Hulda closed her eyes. In a twilight world between sleep and wake, she saw the floor as a dark glass with the image of the car reversed below them and keeping pace. With a difference though. Looking out to see the reflection, she could make out the exact detail of the underside of the car and through the transparent flooring, she could see that Fletcher was in the pilot seat. But by some optical trick that was outside experience, she realized that her own reflection was not there. Nor was Galloway's who should have shown up in the seat next to the pilot.

Gimel-Sin was obscured by an opaque piece of decking, until he came forward to check out progress on the instrument cluster. One part of her mind registered that he had walked the length of the car and was now standing on the same clear patch that supported the pilot's chair, another part was grappling with the knowledge that in the reflection, Fletcher was still alone.

When the car stopped and Fletcher's concentration slackened, she had a momentary newsflash of what was going on in his mind. This time, he was expecting something from the city behind the barrier. He was going to show them something that would surprise them. He was out longer, before the blank screen moved into its niche, and they could see that he had walked ahead on to the flyover and was looking at the far wall of the cave.

It needed no crystal ball to judge that what he saw was other than he had expected.

Hulda had been right in thinking that he had not seen the previous mural in any detail. Dag Fletcher had only seen the girl and could not have described anything else. This time, however, her distracting image was not on the set and he was seeing the decorations with an unbiased eye.

At first, he could not believe that it was the fresco that he had seen before. A seven metre wide strip had been ground to a flat, even surface to run the whole distance round the perimeter. Altogether, the picture was several kilometres long and ran behind the buildings that stood round the square. It was filled with scenes from the life of a busy people. Scenes which had been remembered from the ancient time, when the surface of Plantos Three had been habitable.

The discontinuity caused by the screening buildings made the impact more dramatic. It emphasized that it was all happening, whether in sight or not. Colour was bright as the day it was painted. Figures were in bas-relief, the ultimate in realism.

As he recalled it, the dominant themes had been simple—harvest, hunting, the countryside and a whole botanical register of the vanished flora of the upper world. Now the scene was orgiastic, crowded, with a thread of sadistic savagery.

He remembered a hunting episode, where a group of elegant warriors, like the ancient Masai of Earth planet, had been shown running over open ground to attack an embattled bison with flaring nostrils and pawing hoofs. Now the hunt was a maddened rout and the quarry was a frantic girl, with sweat glistening on her naked back, looking over her shoulder to check out how near they were and to give the artist a free hand in showing a full face fractured by terror.

Hulda came up beside him and said, 'Is this what you wanted us to see?'

Fletcher was too disturbed to notice that she had been at it again. He took the question on its merits. 'Not this. This I do not understand. It would take decades to produce a fresco this size. How could it be changed?'

'Perhaps you do not remember well enough?'

'I remember.'

'They say you can see anything you want to see on a blank wall. Perhaps you are projecting the picture.'

'Thank you very much. If I have a mind like that, you'd do well to keep out of it. Your wandering Psyche might get ambushed.'

'It makes Gimel-Sin's point. This is no place to be.'

'But you saw the girl back there. Where does she fit in?'

'I can't help you. I can only say I don't see her the way you do. She fits in all right.'

Fletcher thought, 'Why does she say that? What motive can she have for twisting the truth? But then, it would be stupid to expect an objective assessment of one woman from another. She's a totally different type. Just wouldn't appreciate her.'

Getting the gist of it, Hulda moved impatiently away. She had a momentary urge to beat him over the head with a club. Political training paid off. From a ten-metre start towards the car, she said, 'I think we should get on, Commander.'

The last barrier was in front of them before they expected it. Fifteen kilometres of straight road, with brilliant light, allowed Fletcher to give the car its head. They went through with a bow wave of compressed air and a rising scream from the power pack. At journey's end, Gimel-Sin was first out and fairly hopped from one foot to the other, while Fletcher searched for the place to make a cut. Moved by a sense of occasion, Hulda and Galloway joined the other two on the floor of the roadway and came in for a command which made little sense; but which was delivered with a whiplash crack that had them following it without question.

Fletcher felt the bulkhead moving against his hands and reacted as he had done once before, when he had known that Fingalnan artillery was waiting to blast him from the other side. He snapped out, 'Get down. Flat.'

Gimel-Sin's military training took him first to the parquet by a nonasecond, with Hulda a bad third. Fletcher flattened her the last half metre and was lying half across her like a protective rug, when the screen slotted itself silently overhead and the way was open.

No destructive blast funnelled down the tube. On the count of ten, taken to pulse beats of the pneumatic cushion under his hand, Fletcher cautiously raised his head. Then he stood up and pulled Hulda after him. They made a line across the mouth of the tunnel looking down into the city.

It was the biggest yet; obviously, the metropolis of the system. Impressive as it was, there was another human artifact that was making its bid for attention. In the centre of the immense piazza, the Fingalnan supership *Leviathon* was standing on its tripod jacks all of three hundred metres high and shining as though newly burnished for a commissioning ceremony. Of the debris and general air of smash that had characterized the square on his last sight of it, Fletcher could see no sign.

His surprise was a pale, wan thing compared with the Fingalnan's. Gimel-Sin had been aboard, when *Petrel's* scout car had homed like a flying bomb on the number one tripod and every internal alarm had gone into frenetic clamour. He remembered getting out in the seconds when the canting ship had gone into an unstoppable fall that had killed thirty of the crew and smashed every plate on the impact side from the power pack to the cone.

A high rate of discharge among the synapses pushed out a harmonic that Hulda could receive. It was genuine. Impassive on the outside, he was, nevertheless, clocking up the full gamut of stupefaction on his personal affectometer.

It meant nothing to Galloway except that it was the last pad he could expect to find a viable spacer on. Less committed than the rest, he said, 'That's a fine ship. There's no denyin' that fact. A trifle narrow in the waist for all that height, but a very fine bit of buildin', and that's the truth.'

To anyone for whom the existence of a rose was violence, it would have been the banality of all time. Seemingly there were none about. Fletcher said soberly, 'You can say that again, Jock. The question is who did the building. I'll be surprised, if what we've come to find is still there. But having come so far, we might as well look. We shall have to take the car to reach the entry port. Gimel-Sin will go aboard with me. Take the pilot slot, Jock and when we get inside stand off and cruise about on this side, until I signal we want to be taken off. Commissar Hulda will stay here and wait.'

'Why?'—Hulda was not keen to go, but having come so far she reckoned she ought to go the whole way.

'It may be a trap.'

'If they trap you, I cannot walk back to *Konstet*.'

'You will at least have some sort of chance.'

The words were plain enough in the context and the hidden mental gloss made it even clearer. He knew she carried as all space personnel did, the instant passport to release for use in situations where any rational organism would elect to die. Oblivion pill, one, for the use of. . . .

It could be that a sophisticated enemy would find a way to prevent her using it. But out here, in the wings, she would have time to judge what was going on and make a choice.

There was also an element of determination. Argument would get her nowhere. He had made up his mind and that was it.

Hulda said, 'Very well,' and walked out to a natural observation point on the flyover. She leaned on a metre-high parapet to look down into a piazza that glittered with blue, silver and gold in an intricate mosaic. The car passed her with a down draught that sent her pale bell of hair swirling round her head and flattened her pants against the back of her legs.

She thought of the faces on the fresco and on the mural in the first city. Faces were the history of a people. They were the distilled essence of what the dialectic of environment and heredity had produced over a period. The car planed across her line of sight and she watched Galloway bring it to a nicely-judged stop at the entry port.

Fletcher and Gimel-Sin disappeared through the hatch. The car sidled away, circled the ship and kept station a hundred metres off.

Nothing moved, either in the wide, empty square with its ornate pavements or the tall colourful buildings. Time passed. Five, ten, fifteen minutes on her time disk. Then she saw an elevator platform on a shining central spindle drop slowly between the tripod legs.

Distance was too great for detail, but she recognized the tall figure as Fletcher's. When the tray hit floor level, he walked into the square, looking along the ground. He was still obsessed by his black witch. Fifty metres out, he stopped and looked up at the ship, then knelt down to take a closer look at the mosaic work at his feet.

Hulda moved impatiently. Behind her, there was a definitive click and she checked out the tunnel barrier. It had fallen into place. She spun round to call out and alert Fletcher.

He was no longer there. In the split second it had taken to turn her head, he had vanished as though by legerdemain.

The car was planing down to where Gimel-Sin was making an urgent mime to be picked up. Then the set filled as if for a musical finale with figures that a pattern-seeking mind sorted into three types. The majority were Fingalnans, one minority group owed origin to Earth planet. The rest, less than half a dozen, were animated versions of the Plantos mural, and, in spite of barbaric undress, were clearly the overseers of the enterprise.

Chapter Seven

Trudy Brogan, on anchor watch as executive in charge, reckoned that if anything could reconcile her to leaving the service and settling for a skillet, it was the limbo they were now in. It was no help either to have Fingalnans at the navigation and power desks. She missed the reassurances of Pete Bramah's dark head across the cabin. The two small, silvery aliens were correct and professional and obviously knew everything there was to know about the job, but they gave her the green creeps.

Metabolism had something to do with it. Body heat was well above Earth level. It was like standing near a mobile heating unit when she went over to the main scanner to run the half-hourly sweep of the arc of sky above the ship.

Kronor—the navigation number three—but a full commander by rank—was watching every move she made, whether out of professional curiosity or simple lust she could not decide, but it made her clumsy. That, and the persistent pressure that Simpson was putting on. She wondered how long she could fend him off without alerting Bramah to the dilemma she was in.

As a consequence, she sent out a surge of power that doubled the range of the beam and put up a warning light on the panel to tell her that she was going the right way to burn out the gear.

Kronor whipped out of his swivel chair and put a hot restraining hand on her bare arm. Then they both held still, caught by the faint image that had come up on the screen.

At extreme range and too etiolated for identification, there was the unmistakable shadow of a stationary ship.

There was nothing wrong with the Fingalnan's reflexes.

Before she had read off the fix on the hairline grid, he had whipped back to his console and keyed the general alarm.

Crewmen lumbered into the control cabin, shooting the last seals on space gear. With Simpson gyrating slowly on the command island, she was free to dig her own suit from the storage bin under her desk and start sealing up, conscious that the next move was due from her section.

In the absence of Furvil, the communications number three, Barlac, was already setting up a fixed direction beam from the data and she was able to report, in the fastest time of her career, that communications was all buttoned up.

Every subsidiary screen took the picture. There was no doubt that *Konstet* was in trouble. Sitting plumb in a parking orbit, where she could blast anything that moved, was a spacer of a type that Trudy Brogan could not identify, except to say that it was unlikely to be a commercial ship.

Barlac had no doubts. He said, 'Communications Three to Commander. Scotian cruiser, seventy degrees of arc precisely. Stationary as of now.'

Fergus, who had come in to replace Galloway on the power desk, added a civilian gloss, 'Holy cow, she's two-thirds power pack, she'd be down here before we could move our own length.'

It was no help and it had already occurred to Simpson. He could picture the activity in the command cabin of the capital ship. A craft that size would have a computer spread to rival a regional admin centre. Staff types would be sitting on their fannies watching the planet below being shredded down to tennis court strips for analysis. *Konstet* would stick out like an obelisk on a lawn. Any time at all, it could happen. If he moved, it would happen sooner and long before *Konstet's* armament was within effective range, the cruiser could disperse them as instant mist.

It was the classic gambit. Caught, where any commander would aim to catch a quarry. The fact that there was no war on made no difference. Simpson had seen enough of such actions to know that it was a terminal situation. He could not save the ship. Indeed it was unlikely that he could save its personnel.

A lot would depend on the Scotian's aim. If it was to stop their project, he could expect an attack. If it was to intercept and channel the end product another way, they might talk first and deliver an ultimatum. On the whole, though, the second would only be a stage towards the first. Once a Scotian had got what he wanted, he would go for the destruction bit by simple reflex.

Taking it from there, he could expect a wide area of devastation round the ship. Biological damage up to a hundred kilometres. The only transport left to them was the freight trolley and a couple of flat baggage drays. It would take four or five hours in this terrain to get to an area that gave a fifty per cent chance. What they needed was an underground blockhouse.

Fletcher had left his objective marked up on the chart. It was well within the limits for blast and fall out. But underground. That was the answer, staring him in the face. Join the advance party in the tunnel system, with enough supplies to sweat it out for six months and wait for I.G.O. to cotton on to it and send the squadron to investigate.

Five seconds later, he had a rough line of talk mapped out and he began to speak on the general net.

Except for the three Europeans, who had the same regard for logic, there was no immediate sell out. There was a fatalistic streak in the Fingalnans, that made them inclined to sit tight and go for the remote chance that the Scotian computers would miss their hectare.

Finally Simpson said, 'Everybody on the ground ready to move off in four minutes flat.'

Konstet became a termite pillar of ordered chaos. With twenty seconds to spare, Fergus drove the diminutive waggon train from under the tripod and set the trolley's hooded direction finder for the course. If it had a fraction of a degree of error, they were lined up for fifteen thousand kilometres of wilderness that would make McMurdo Sound look like a Polynesian pleasure garden.

Bramah had shipped hoop rails fore and aft on the trucks and had gotten himself strategically wedged with Trudy Brogan on the middle unit. Simpson came down with the sections of a survival dome as the last outgoing load and the elevator whipped back.

It was only then, that he realized that there was not a Fingalnan in sight, after each of the last few loads, one or more had gone back with the empty elevator. Confirmation of the tactic came in a tangible rush of heated gas, beating down on the pad. They were going through the pre-heating drill to warm up the tubes.

One thing was plain. The underside of a ship preparing to move was no place to be. Fergus poured in a little power and the half-track bucketed over hummocky ice towards the polar night.

He held on for two hundred metres, probing into a horseshoe outcrop of rock that hid *Konstet* except for a small triangle of cone. Beyond the ship was a distant bar of yellow, the petrified, unmoving dawn of Plantos. Light grew in an orange nimbus round the stark profile of the crag and the ship began to move.

Slowly, and then with gathering speed, the long, silver column jacked itself out of the twilight zone. The brilliant fishtail of flame burned to an intense cadmium yellow that lit the set and brought every colour in the spectrum from the reflecting ice.

Pete Bramah had an intercom line to his partner and said, 'Maybe Simpson had the wrong angle. They might just do it. Perhaps we should have stayed with the ship.'

The same thought had occurred to the Commodore. Accustomed for many years to make decision at staff level, where the consequences had no personal repercussion, he was now beginning to doubt the wisdom of the old command adage,

'When in doubt give an order. Any order is better than none.'

There was also professional status. If the Fingalnans brought it off, his own estimate of the situation had been badly wrong. It would look very nasty on his record profile.

Konstet was pulling away now under full thrust. She was going to make it. Kronor would probably go on to Cappodan and tell his tale to the Fingalnan consulate there. It would depend on what tale he told. If he invented one that gave a reasonable explanation for the loss of all Earth personnel, I.G.O. might not investigate at all. They would be content that the Fingalnan attempt to get the safe out of *Leviathon* had been abandoned.

Speculation stopped. It had become academic. Where *Konstet* had been, a silver rod with a delicate tail of flame, there was a white asterisk.

There was no need to mime urgently for the others to get down. Each of the three had followed the ship every centimetre of the way. Bramah butted the girl off of the seat and lay with his visor against hers in the shadow of the load. For a nonasecond, the darkside of Plantos was lit as though by a magnesium flash. Then the shock wave tried to tear them from a surface that was ten centimetres deep in running water.

Thinking one thought at a time, Fergus waded back to the half track and checked out the motor. It was still in business, so he moved it along in a slow circle, through the reforming ice. Other than that he was out of programme.

On the second circuit, with the surface solid again, his single beam headlamp picked out a vaudeville team thumbing for a ride. After almost leaving it too late to break free, Bramah and Trudy Brogan had found that the only way to stay out of trouble was to link arms and do a high-knee-raise routine. Even in low gravity, it was a wearing exercise and they had nothing to spare to think about the rest of the party.

They jumped smartly for the footplate and recognized

the driver of the Cannonball as Fergus.

Bramah plugged in for sound and asked without much enthusiasm, 'Where's God's Gift, then?'

The sound of a human voice beating round the inside of his visor brought Fergus back to the here and now, 'Simpson? I don't know. Didn't see him. Wasn't he near you?' He cut power and slid to a halt. Then he lifted the lamp from its bracket and searched around.

Trudy Brogan said, 'We can't leave him. Not in a place like this'—the qualification was necessary for Bramah, who was ready to accept that it was an ill wind and push on.

When they found him, it was still a legitimate point of view. A freak surge of blast had picked the eager Commodore off his feet and beached him on a low ledge of the far wall of the horseshoe spur, like a dinghy left in the fork of a tree after a hurricane.

He was rated as living by the colour code on his gorgette and the air gauge was making a strong, regular kick; but his eyes were closed and there was a livid streak across his forehead where instant deceleration had beaten the ergonomics of his suit.

Other than set up the survival dome and camp on the spot, there was nothing to be done. Bramah reckoned the claims of humanity had been met if they took him along. So they chocked him on the second dray, feet and head overlapping the load and picked up the course for Fletcher's tumulus.

Bramah considered some of the angles. On the surface it would take time, with detours for ground features. One, perhaps two days. Make an early stop on the first leg, put up a dome and take a look at Simpson. No special problem, if the gear stood the strain. Just a certain amount of care. God, they were used to that. Every trip in a spacer was an act of faith in the men who had built the equipment.

He reached out and patted Trudy Brogan's corrugated arm. Her visor turned his way. Dome lamps illuminated each for the other, like rare deep sea neon fish. Her face was pale and unsmiling behind its glass. It was no place for a girl's face to be, when you got right down to it. Bramah thought, 'If we get out of this, I'll make her pack it in, even if it means taking a shore job myself.'

Not being gifted with Hulda's special perception, Trudy Brogan had to take what comfort there was from simple visual clues. After the patting sequence, Bramah lifted a gauntlet with the thumb sticking up and seemed to be saying 'cheese' to the inside of his visor.

She rewarded a trier by returning the compliment, two spectators at a bizarre agricultural show. Any other concessions to human solidarity would have to wait until they got inside the dome. The miniature train ground on at ten kilometres in the hour. Nothing was said. There was nothing to say.

Shortage of anything to say was never a problem with Chairman Paul V. Spencer. He was adept at making a little go a long way and had spent more hours than were consistent with the good life in grinding the corporate ears off of many a committee by polysyllabic repetition of some simple item that was already painfully clear to one and all. It was a method which he had raised to the status of a refined technique.

Nothing was more calculated to make his professional advisers' flesh creep and lead seep into their veins than his standard opening for a long spiel from the chair—'What you are saying, as I understand it, is, briefly . . .'

By the time he was through with it, nobody cared any more and he got his way on the nod, without having to ask for a show of hands.

He was limited a little by cost, when speaking to Halewood over the satellite relay system that linked him with Fingalna; but habit died hard and the acting manager of the trading post could only get in an occasional phrase.

On the use of a Fingalnan ship for the mission to Cappodan

Spencer was forthright. 'What's wrong with *Callisto?* I only hope he knows what he's doing. There's something behind all this generosity. I don't trust them. What's the latest bulletin? What was the latest position?—Don't tell me, I'll get it from the daily indicator. It's a relief to me to know that Varley's in the area. With all the taxes we pay, we ought to get a little protection. Well, keep me in the picture. I'll talk to you again in forty-eight hours.'

Half an hour later, the large empurpled mug was filling the screen to the brim and Halewood reckoned he was missing the sanctity of deep space.

Spencer said, 'You didn't tell me that it's two days since *Konstet* checked in a position. What's Fletcher up to?'

'Nothing out-of-the-way, Chairman. As you know, he's got Commissar Hulda and a staff officer from the squadron along. If there was anything wrong with the ship, the auto beacon would have stopped sending out its signal. It's still putting up the "on passage" light at Argentus control.'

'I didn't think he could have lost the ship in an empty quarter. It's a tenderfoot run to Cappodan. A blind baby with no arms could do it on its head. He's gone off course and he doesn't want me to know where he is, until it suits him. I know Fletcher too well. When you get to speak with him, tell him that he's running a commercial service not a comic mystery tour. He'll go too far one of these days and he'll be out. On the beach. I wouldn't trust him to take a garbage truck straight to a dump.'

When Halewood called back five hours later, Spencer was apoplectic. 'You've got me out of my bed, captain. What is it, then?'

'Argentus have reported that there is no signal from *Konstet.*'

'What about Cappodan?'

'No signal.'

'Faded out?'

'Went out at full strength.'

Spencer looked tired. Halewood thought, 'In spite of all the bluster, the old bastard really feels it. The buck really stops at his desk.'

'All right, captain. There's nothing we can do about it. Who has he with him?'

'Bramah, Galloway, Brogan, Fergus. Plus the two super-cargo.'

'Does I.G.O. know?'

'Yes.'

'Very well. Hold the next-of-kin signal for twenty-four hours. It's just possible there's a mechanical failure. And Captain.'

'Yes.'

'I'm sorry.'

'I understand that, Chairman.'

Spencer's face faded with the screen and then reassembled itself as a visual afterthought.

'What's the Fingalnan reaction?'

'Nothing yet.'

'Keep me informed.'

'Check.'

Although none of it had spilled over to the European Space office, the Fingalnan response was blocking switchboards in the higher echelons of government. Within fifteen minutes of *Konstet's* candle blowing out, Administrator Veck was defending his corner at a select meeting in the President's penthouse suite.

There were five present. Xantu—a dessicated mandarin in full military regalia representing the military arm; Dumuzu, the minister for interplanetary affairs; Urur, the youngest minister in the government and the one regarded as the main spring of the war party, given general oversight of long-term economic planning; and President Tylon himself who was inclined to speak with some resentment as one who had been pushed into an untenable situation by incompetent advisers.

Tylon said, 'As I see it, the affair has been mismanaged. Bringing in outsiders was an error of judgement. Now there will be an investigation. Theoretically the ship belongs to European Space and their Chairman is already pushing I.G.O. to send a search team along the route. There is a powerful squadron in the area. I have no doubt that the request will be taken up. Plantos will come under scrutiny.'

Veck said, 'With respect, President, I do not see that this is any more dangerous than it has always been. We do not know that the ship reached Plantos—though I would say that it was likely. However, a fault of this nature would indicate that she had been totally destroyed, in which case there will be no survivors. Nothing about the nature of the quest will be revealed to I.G.O. I say nothing will be revealed to I.G.O.'

As the military expert, Admiral Xantu felt that Veck had taken some of his ground. He snapped, 'Repeating the assurance does not make it true, Administrator. Unluckily, this I.G.O. fleet is the one which carried out the action on Plantos. Varley has a long memory. He will want to know why this ship made a detour to such a place. There is virtually only one reason why a Fingalnan ship should call there. It has to be connected with the wreck of *Leviathon*. They will do the sum and realize that there is something remaining that we have an interest in and they will sift every kilo of scrap.'

Tylon said, 'Do you have any theory about what has happened to the ship, Admiral?'

'It is my belief that she was destroyed by enemy action. *Konstet* was in fine condition. Every millimetre of her fabric was checked and double checked. For months, the maintenance units have been preparing her for this mission. It is utterly unlikely that she would suffer any kind of structural or mechanical failure. Also, she is as up-to-the-minute, equipment-wise, as any unit in service with any fleet. She could not have been surprised and attacked in open flight. Not even by a supership. In those conditions, she could have identified a hostile and taken avoiding action.'

Administrator Urur made no gain in the popularity stakes by interposing, 'There is always the human factor, Admiral. A ship or an institution is only as strong as the men who operate it.'

Xantu never liked pushers and a young pusher was well over the edge; he said coldly, 'The crew were hand picked. Every man is a commander by rank and dedicated to the service. I have every confidence in the men and the machine. If I may go on, without uninformed commentary, I would say that *Konstet* was on the ground and was attacked by a ship of vastly superior armament. If it had been anything smaller than a cruiser she could have taken off and kept out of range.

'Now if she was caught on the ground, she must have reached Plantos. It is even possible that the mission was accomplished and she was ready to go on to Cappodan. I leave others with diplomatic skill to amplify that and consider the implications.'

There was a digestive pause and Veck took up the running with, 'From a security point of view the last possibility is the most acceptable. That way, the episode is closed and all traces destroyed. But as I see it, following the Admiral's excellent hypothesis, it is just as likely that a landing party from *Konstet* was out on location at the time and is still there. Then we must assume that the hostile ship could land and pick them up with whatever they were able to find. If, however, the hostile believed that he had successfully neutralized the whole of the personnel with the ship, he might retire from the area. Then, any landing party would eventually be picked up by the I.G.O. inquiry team. We can not afford to accept that any one of these possibilities is the correct one. I say not one of these explanations could be relied on.'

Making a first contribution, Dumuzu added another

sombre strand to the web, 'It has always been possible that I.G.O. intelligence knew, or suspected, that there was in existence a treaty document. I think we should now accept that they have hit on the likelihood of a copy being carried by the flagship of the alliance. Coincidence should never be dismissed at face value. When the I.G.O. fleet appeared in this area, I alerted every agent we have in I.G.O. capitals. It seems to me, that, if we had not made this attempt to reach *Leviathon*, they would have done it themselves on one pretext or another. As it is, they went along with the project, so that we could pull the chestnut out of the fire for them.

'But a further fact has come from the agents' reports. Scotia has been busy on her own account. There is reliable evidence that a Scotian ship is missing without trace, although there has been no general release of this information. Also, a Scotian cruiser left Lados with no destination announced.

'I need not weigh my words in this company. Scotia is a dangerous ally. It is not beyond possibility that she would act independently in this matter. The treaty document would be a powerful blackmail weapon. Many neutral planets would pay through the nose, rather than have a close investigation by I.G.O.'

Tylon said, 'I appreciate the last point. I am sure all here take that view. Though, for military reasons, the Scotian alliance is an important one. This is a delicate and complicated matter. No O.G.A planet is strong enough to risk a confrontation with I.G.O. at this point in time. Is there any positive suggestion?'

Xantu said, 'It would test I.G.O. reaction, if we request permission to use another ship to check out the route. After all, it was a charter flight by this government. Indeed *not* to make such a request would be suspicious. I will brief a corvette, which complies with the commission's restrictions on armament and have it ready to go within the hour. Do not reveal this, but I will accompany her myself.'

A murmur of agreement came from the council. Dumuzu

said, 'I am sure they will agree. They are not anxious to provoke an open breach. Once on Plantos, you will be able to make your own assessment of the situation.'

One already ashore on Circe's island was making an assessment of a situation which he believed had got as bizarre as it could well get.

Fletcher experienced a turning moment, which sent him to the limit of G tolerance, and felt that he was clinging fly-like to the floor which had momentarily become a ceiling. When his head cleared, he was still kneeling on the parquet, but the figure of the dark girl was no longer spread out for inspection. Instead, he was looking at a pair of feet in white heel-less sandals, with thongs outlining a brown and finely-turned leg.

Ever a thoughtful student of the female patella, Fletcher put the pair, ten centimetres in front of his incredulous eyes, as grade one examples of the genre. Still trying to figure it out, he stayed on hands and knees like a hound dog and craned back his head to take in the full figure.

The promise of the feet was fulfilled with every kind of bonus. It was a girl, who contrived to have an individual presence and combine with it the archetype of the female idea. A fine bronze chain, low on the hips, supported a neat triangle of apricot fabric with a stylized design of lotus flowers picked out in silver thread. That and a dime sized navel jewel was all the concession she was making to haute couture; but it was plainly enough. Anything else would have been wasted art.

Fletcher suddenly realized that he was still taking a dog's eye view of the phenomenon and pulled himself to his feet. Positions were to some extent reversed, her eyes were level with his chin and she had to look up at him.

Epstein eyes like black milk. Elongated, kohl-rimmed; lids an unexpected brilliant peacock-blue. Hair, seen in 3-D, had a blue lustre which had beaten the artist. Fletcher, trying for a touchstone, to establish whether or not he had, in fact, joined the majority group of the dead, put out his hands, as though expecting they would go through the image and prove it to be a mirage.

They made contact with shoulders that were cool and smooth as polished stone and she obligingly took a step forward to show that any similarity with a graven image ended there. Firm breasts nudged pneumatically at his lower ribs. There was no longer any reasonable doubt that she was flesh and blood. Well, flesh at the least count.

Fletcher recoiled discourteously as though bitten by an adder and she said, using speech tones, 'What is it, Commander, do you not recognize me?'

In some ways, he reckoned that he recognized her too well. As one builds up a concept of a table from all the tables that appear in experience, so that any new example can be identified, and yet never precisely define the ideal table as a real object; so there was the nebulous, background notion of a woman.

This one was his private concept externalized. The word made flesh. It was as if his mind had undergone major surgery and was still suffering from post-operative shock.

By an effort of will, Fletcher forced himself to take in the rest of the set. That too was familiar. It duplicated the city square he had been in. It *was* the square. Except that one important item did not figure. There was no sign of *Leviathon*.

Doubt crowded him again and he looked back at the girl. Correctly interpreting his problem she said, 'You are surprised that you do not see the ship. It is not easy for you to understand, but you have travelled enough to know that there are many modes of existence. Matter can be arranged in many ways. Mind is the ultimate engineer. We discovered that aeons ago.'

'Who are you?'

'I am Tallou. *We* are the survivors of the ancient people of Plantos, who were space travellers before your planet of

Earth had the beginnings of human life. We have forgotten more than you will know for millennia to come.'

Dag Fletcher was bemused, but he had not capitulated at all levels. He had seen many cultures at many stages of development. Taking the claims of an advanced group too seriously led to psychological discouragement. A man was a man was a man, period. He had to operate on the level he was at and stand or fall by his own systems of reference. 'We do all right. Just tell me the score. I'll understand well enough.'

'First I will take you to the synod. It will be a good moment for me. It justifies my belief that you would return and that, when you did, you would look at my picture in the square. A great deal of the available power was concentrated at that place. There were some who wished to use it elsewhere; but there is very little left and what there is must be husbanded to take the rest of our people through into the other reality.'

'That makes it all crystal clear. But why me? Why do you want me on this side, wherever that is?'

'Come.'

The verbal invitation was amplified by the way she walked ahead. Any male mummy would have left its sarcophagus and hopped in her wake as if in a resurrection sack race. Fletcher thought, 'I don't get within a good sea mile of what goes on; but what can I lose?'

He followed, ten metres to the rear, through a stretch of ornamental garden with a fountain that made the warm air damp and set glistening droplets of water on her bare back. Tallou took no notice and kept a straight, if undulating, course for the porch of a tall building block that glowed with colour like a peacock's tail.

When he reached the inner lobby, it was empty; but a large, double-leaf door to the left was wide open. He went on in, and was the focal point for a circle, which seemed more in line with the remodelled fresco of the last city than anything yet. It was enough to have him unclip the laser from his belt.

It was an action that drew an appreciative laugh from all

present, except Tallou who had gone to stand beside the centre console of a half-circle that faced the door. She was looking at him, with the simple pride of a hunter who had pitched a fat buck on the family hearth and wanted the group to give her a big hand.

Fletcher had his diffident streak and at no time believed that he was, personally, the pin round which the galaxy revolved; but the laughter had a harmonic of malice in it that grated on his nerves. After all, they were not so secure in human superiority. At a quick estimate, there could be a dozen. Men and women about equal. Like Tallou, they appeared to be naked to the waist, though most carried an assortment of personal jewellery; broad armbands of electrum; gold collars in square or oblong links, elaborate necklaces of cornelian and lapis lazuli; ornate finger rings; all glowing with a hard brilliance in the shadowless light. But features had a blunted, atavistic look. A coinage from worn dies. Apes playing with abandoned human equipment.

He used the formal phrases that he had flipped out like a visa on many a planetfall, 'Commander Fletcher of the I.G.O. ship *Konstet*. If you co-operate with me you will come to no harm. I want to know the purpose of the rebuilding of the ship in the square and what you have done to bring me to this place.'

It was pompous, but not funny enough to get another laugh. The man in the middle, where Tallou was, sat still and writhed back his lips.

Fletcher brought up the laser and aimed for a stucco figurine on a niche in the rear wall above the man's head. Maybe a Napoleonic whiff of grapeshot would make a point better than a long speech.

He had a confused nonasecond, when Tallou's face seemed to be in a state of flux, as though rapidly alternating between the face of the picture and one more in line with the rest of the group. But before he could establish which was the true and definitive edition, he was below ground level.

A square metre of floor had whipped away from under his

feet and gravity had pulled him smartly into a narrow pit. Only cat-like reflexes kept him from cracking his forehead on the facing wall.

The lid stayed off and acoustic screening was not so complete that he missed out on noises from up aloft. There was no doubt, he was making their day.

Chapter Eight

Commissar Hulda ran for the fallen shutter. Not naturally a technocrat, she had forced herself to understand at least the operative side of most of the equipment that advanced societies had dreamed up. Five seconds concentration on the switchgear made its modus operandi plain enough. The crunch came when she threw over the right levers and there was no joy from the porcelain curtain.

She spent another minute checking it out and realized that a master circuit had overridden the local panel. Only a demolition party could break out.

Running back along the flyover, she was reminded of the fresco. Flight invites pursuit. Although the level remained empty, she had a feeling that she was being watched and any minute a baying hound might materialize out of the fabric. She slowed to a walk and then stopped in the centre of the roadway, a splash of lime-green against the prevailing silver-grey.

The car appeared, away over by the crescent of buildings, climbing and turning towards her. She waved and then stood still. Galloway was making for the tunnel and had to come her way.

The car planed down between her and the exit and she had a sudden knowledge that, if it had been open, it would have gone on without her. That meant that Gimel-Sin was in charge.

Hulda reached the hatch as Galloway climbed out, obviously sent to open the gate. He looked disillusioned as a reluctant gardener who has stubbed a toe on a concrete gnome. 'It's that wee silver bastard, Commissar. He's got the only armament in the shop. I'd have gone down to look for the commander. Mind you, it's no go. We couldna' do a blind thing against that lot.'

'I understand. There is nothing we can do. It would be wisest to get back. I.G.O. will send a task force to see what is being done here. But we cannot use this exit. I have already tried.'

Gimel-Sin appeared in the hatch with a riot gun that looked too big for him. His eyes were bleak. He was outside the scope of reason. Going back without success would be a terminal exercise. He said, 'Get on, Earthman. Raise the barrier.'

Hulda reckoned he was in no mood to take in another negative report, and watched with him, while Galloway made his unnecessary journey.

'Well?'

'It's no possible.'

At the same moment, a group of men appeared round the curve of the road, Earthmen and Fingalnans, six abreast, four or five deep, spread across the width, running at a jog trot.

Before either of them could move, Gimel-Sin had whipped inside, and slammed the door. The car rose two metres and began to turn in its own length. With the posse less than fifty metres distant, the car accelerated at full thrust, its under-slung multiple laser cutting a swathe through the column.

They still came on. Briefing had been deep. Some on hands and knees, some writhing like wounded snakes; with every kind of injury, they came on.

Except for a suicide leap from the flyover, there was nowhere to go. Back to the barrier, Hulda heard herself begin to scream as a thick-set Earthman, bleeding like a colander, grabbed for her with one good arm.

Emotion sent a brief surge of psychokinetic energy ranging round the set. Two thoughts vied for precedence in her head, before she blacked out. One was a realization that the blank look in the man's eyes had nothing to do with the traumatic shock of being in a terminal condition, there was no mind there to feel that kind of concern. The other was that she had left it late to swallow her own passport to oblivion.

Dag Fletcher picked up the transmission in his narrow cell and correctly assessed that Hulda was in trouble. It was no more than a newsflash and he was left looking at the wall half a metre in front of his eyes.

There was, in any event, little he could do about it. The laser had dropped in with him and he picked it up and shoved it back in its clip. Then he reached for the lip of the pit and drew himself up to look over the edge like any mandrake.

This time, when he might reasonably have expected it, there was no laughter from the Plantosians. Instead, a man who had been squatting just out of sight, leaned forward and struck him open handed across the side of his face with enough force to make him lose his grip.

It was a more humiliating blow than if it had been with a clenched fist. It was contemptuous, as though they regarded him as a child.

Fletcher set his teeth and tried again. This time, he took the weight mainly on his left arm. As the hand came across to strike, he grabbed for it with his right and brought the striker down with him into the pit.

It was like pulling a shark into a dinghy. For ten confused seconds, there was an explosion of force as the man thrashed about to get himself right way up and regain the initiative. When the situation stabilized, he was flat against a wall with a knee grinding into his crotch and an arm pinned across his throat.

He craned his head forward and Fletcher smacked it back against the tiling. At the same time, the Earthman called up the shaft. 'Does anybody care about this gorilla? If you want him alive, you have five seconds to say so.'

Counting aloud, he put an extra unit of pressure on the neck for every number. At four, the man's eyes were bulging and a mottled look was gathering under the pale brown skin. The light overhead dimmed and Tallou leaned head and shoulders into the opening.

Even in the stressed situation, Fletcher had to concede that it was a very photogenic angle. Rimlit, from the light behind her, with eyes brilliant in her own shadow. She seemed totally out of place among these people. She said, 'Commander.'

'What is it?'

'Release him. We have got away to a bad start with you. Let him go and we will explain why you have been brought here.'

'How do I get out?'

'Wait.'

She moved lithely out of vision and Fletcher could feel movement in the wall at the man's back. The whole floor was rising. As it levelled with the surface, the man fell and then rolled clear.

Fletcher thought, 'God, I'm simple. All set up like a clay pigeon.'

In his absence below deck, there had been a change. The consoles had grown in height by the addition of an oblong flap with a small slot for viewing the interrogee. There was nobody in sight to pick out as a target. But the laughter had stopped. He said, 'Tallou?'

The leading hand replied for her. 'Resistance is useless, Commander. At any time we could have killed you. Make no mistake about that. If you want to live, you must do as you are told.'

'You have gone to a lot of trouble to get me here. That argues that you need my help in some way. You are not going the right way to get it. Let me tell you this, as soon as it is known that my ship is delayed, there will be other craft sent to investigate. Craft with power enough to split Plantos into meteorites, if it is believed that you are a threat. What has happened to my companions?'

'Questions, Commander, and threats. Too many. Let us say

that they are still alive. But for how long will depend on you.'

'What do you want me to do?'

'That is better. First you can throw away that weapon. Primitive as it is, it might kill one of us before you were destroyed.'

Fletcher considered it. As a balance of power it was no good to him. The gesture could well be worth it. He had in fact nothing to lose. As he took it from its clip, he thumbed the selector over to its non-lethal setting and pitched it across the floor.

A number of things happened at once. Shutters dropped again and opened the way for fair exchange in vision. Tallou left the side of the leader and came out to pick up the gun. His recent victim, full of bounce and brio, ran from the end stall, with a curved knife held chest high at arm's length and every intention of taking a down payment in blood.

Fletcher was distracted by the general movement and made his play a fraction late. He felt the knife touch across his chest like a thin wire, as he pivoted flat-footed in a classic feint. Then he had the arm in a double grip and dislocated it from the shoulder.

Once started on the sequence, he followed it through, in a short, but thorough, pattern of destruction. When it was over, he found that he had at last made a considerable break-through. From Tallou, round the circle, every eye was appreciative. Loss of numbers might be regretted in principle; but they had enjoyed the spectacle as a small aesthetic pleasure in itself.

Eyes were glistening. Mouths wet. Blunted features were alight. He reckoned he had started something that would be difficult to stop. Once on this tack, they might sacrifice any long-term plan for a present Roman holiday of brutality.

He cooled it by an appeal to Tallou. 'I understand that was not intended. Now can we get down to business? Tell me what you want.'

She switched to reason with an obvious effort, but

addressed the king pin of her own side. 'I am sure he will do what we ask, Tuchulcha. Of course, he is suspicious. We have not done anything to make him otherwise. Let me take him to the observatory and explain our great plan. Then he can come before you again. Operate the link.'

Except for the last bit, it sounded reasonable to Fletcher; but there was a doubtful pause before it got the seal of approval from Tuchulcha. When it came, it was no more than a surly nod.

Tallou did not wait for conviction to wither. She took his arm and walked him towards the right hand wall. As they approached it, iris-eye panels sliced back to leave a circular opening and they stepped through to a white tubular tunnel which appeared to stretch away to indefinite distance. Spiral corrugations gave an illusion of movement. Fletcher said, 'A water's-eye view of an Archimedean screw.'

But she was not listening. Her lips were moving in a private count down that reached its zero when her fingers dug sharply into his arm and the tunnel itself seemed to convulse like a swallowing throat.

When sense data sorted themselves out, they were standing in a circular room that reminded him more than anything of the observation deck of a satellite. Dark panels could have been direct vision viewing ports; the instrumentation on a huge, computer island in the centre could have been a navigation spread.

Four Plantosians were in the room and two things came clear to Fletcher. One was that the enterprise, whatever it was, was short on personnel and the other was a certainty that he was once again on the same plain of reality as the ship *Leviathon*.

Still holding his arm, Tallou led him to the left wing and spoke to an incongruous figure seated in the operator's chair. He had the flat, powerful physique of a climber; but the face that watched them was a misfit, a collection of odd items, the face of an in-bred idiot that should know nothing of the complex hardware it was monitoring.

Again Fletcher wondered why Tallou was different, why of all the Plantosians he had seen she carried the promise of a classically proportioned body to a face that matched it. Her opening words gave him another angle to think about. She said, 'Yarris, this is the navigator who will fly our ship. The synod have allowed me to bring him here, so that he can understand the plan.'

Yarris answered in a tongue that was unfamiliar and seemed to be inclined to argue it out. She replied in the same, but the tone was unmistakable. She was laying it on the line. Whatever his opinion was, he had to do as he was told.

Finally Yarris spoke in speech tones. 'I do not think you are ready for this knowledge. However, I will do my best to explain. Sit beside me and place your hands on this plate as I do. You also Tallou. You can be his guide.'

Dag Fletcher reckoned he had nothing to lose. Without their say-so, he was not going to find his way out of this one. Curiosity in any case was enough. It was time somebody filled in a little detail.

First contact with the surface made him draw back sharply and look at it again. Touch was out of key with vision. What appeared to be a flat sheet of cloudy glass, which he expected to feel hard and cold, was soft and warm as taut skin.

Tallou and Yarris looked at him as though impatient to begin and he replaced his hands. There was a sensation of dissolving warmth that spread up his arms and seemed to invade his body. He knew that if he had not been sitting down, he would have fallen and an instinct of caution made him try to pull free. But it was already too late. Nerve relays had packed up. The incoming tide was irreversible.

Only surrender to it was possible and complete surrender was a relief. He was no longer bound by the small aggregates of experience that made the self. He was not looking out from a certain point in time and experience that added up to a certain person conscious of itself.

Perhaps it was on the screen in front of him, or perhaps it was projected in the holographic web of his own mind, or perhaps he was there in real terms; but he was experiencing the tangible presence of a wide well-paved street. He was in a city dominated by pyramid forms, truncated at the top to give space for soaring, temple-like structures. The ascending planes were interrupted by terraces and gardens. Along every facade, there were elaborate frescoes in brilliant colour.

Altogether, there was a feeling of great mass as though the buildings would endure for ever, that men had created a setting for themselves which was indestructible.

The sky was cloudless and of the palest tint of cerulean blue. Stonework was white, sharp-edged, ageless. The people in the streets and moving on the immense stairways were familiar. Men and women had long, dark hair to shoulder length, cloaks of plain brilliant colour, caught by jewelled clasps on the left shoulder, thonged sandals, short tabards of fine, transparent linen. He was on the surface of Plantos and time was a spatial distance rather than a serial division. Plantos existed still for anyone who knew where to find it.

He saw Tallou ahead and quickened his pace to catch up. She rounded a corner into a shaded alleyway and he blundered into her. She was waiting for him, had seen him and known he was following. Arms went swiftly round his neck. Mouth anemone soft. The world resolved into a relaxed and open O.

Whether it was a bit that the guide had thrown in as a bonus, or whether he had imported the action from his own subconscious, was not clear. In any event there was no progression. The scene dissolved and reformed and he was in the same place in another period. Colour had drained out of the sky, it was a glare that was too bright to be looked at directly. Light had eroded the stone. Corners were rounded and worn, the mass was being ground down to a rubble of desolation.

What people there were moved jerkily in and out of the buildings, like vagrants who were camping on the site of a city that was not their own.

Tallou, unchanged, was walking like a trained dancer along the broad run of the street towards him. The heat of the sun was a burden as though it had liquid weight and was pouring in a heavy stream over his head and shoulders. When she was close, he could see that her skin was finely dewed with sweat and her eyes were dark and enormous.

Without a word, she led him to the nearest ziggurat and they went from intense light into almost total darkness. The great mass of stone insulated them from the heat of the day in an astringent temperature drop and he heard her sharp intake of breath. But before he could touch her, she was ahead, running now down a broad ramp towards a bronze grille with a light behind it.

Clumsy in the sudden cold, she was half a minute struggling with the gear and then they were inside what was near enough a conventional elevator.

In five seconds, they were at a level which was familiar, an underground city complex. So this was the period just before the surface had finally become untenable and preparations had already been made. It could have been any one of the cities. They looked down at the main square from a high balcony. This time, he had a question. 'One thing I have noticed. The people here and before are all much of an age. There are no children and no old people. Why is that?'

'That is one of the things I have to tell you. A long time ago, we developed the technique of cloning.'

'Cloning?'

'Tissue is taken from a person and from it an exact replica of the body can be reproduced. Then a period of one year is allowed for the original to teach the copy what it wishes to retain. Then both are placed in the transfer chamber and the last residue of personality is switched to the new body and the old one is dead.'

'A kind of immortality. What has gone wrong to make the numbers fall?'

'There was always wastage. Every transfer was not successful. Also. . . .' Here she paused and seemed doubtful whether to go on. Then she said quickly, 'Some undesirable traits were strengthened over the years. There was a period of anarchy, when an ancient practice of human sacrifice was revived. Now we are very few and every life has to be husbanded. That is why we avoided contact, when you were last in the city.'

'We searched around. Where did you go?'

'That is another matter I am allowed to disclose. This will be harder for you to believe, because it is outside your experience of reality.'

'Try me.'

'Matter is only solid in a relative degree. To a bird, the air is a medium through which it can travel; to a fish, water is a manageable world. To another form, is it not conceivable, that what appears solid to you could be relatively open in texture?'

She had turned her back to the parapet and was leaning on it with both hands behind her in a pose that was totally at odds with the technical conversation. The low, even voice was stating a theme in counterpoint to what her eyes and body were offering. Fletcher, no slouch in recognizing an affirmative signal, had to strain his brain to keep on the educational tack.

But the drive behind curiosity was more powerful than the drive to sex. Besides, a flash of insight told him with their history, sex would be devalued on Plantos. Take away the necessity for a stable relationship and the possibility of protective tenderness for the woman as a mother of children, and you were left with the small change of sensation for its own sake.

Something of the thought might have passed to Tallou; she twisted round abruptly and presented a back which was hardly less sensational as an erotic object.

Fletcher said, 'So I concede that about matter. Where do we go from there?'

'So long as your mind is not closed to a new idea, you may follow this. The outer skin of Plantos is special in a number of ways. We have exploited that fact. Just as a ship is reflected in water on which it sails, so our underground complex is reflected under the surface of the squares and roadways. By undergoing a certain irradiation, we can adapt to move into the reflection.'

Her caution was justified. Fletcher reckoned he was being told the big lie which is supposedly more convincing than a number of small ones. Maybe he should have settled for sex; but even that, in the convoluted sequence he was in, would be an illusion in an illusion.

He said, 'But the ship is not reflected.'

'There are areas which we can isolate. When you stopped to look at my picture, we had prepared that place so that you could be brought through.'

'And where are we now?'

'We have passed through a membrane in the race history bank. Size is as relative as time. We are within the holographic structure of its memory. What is happening is happening only in your mind.'

Fletcher put his hands on the balcony one on either side of her. For a mental phenomenon, the stone was solid enough. There was a tangible warmth from the smooth body caught in the narrow V. Skin had the pallor of milk in a tinted glass. Partly in the best scientific tradition of one checking out all the angles, he deliberately lowered his head and touched down with his mouth on the nape of her neck.

The machine was doing a good job. If consciousness was the sum of information for an organism, he was getting sense data which could not be disregarded from past references. Skin was unexpectedly cool, hyaline as alabaster and slightly salt. Response was immediate and out of all proportion to the simple act, like shifting a lever and firing a rocket.

Tallou twisted round in the pen, brushing pneumatically against his arms and wrapped herself in a Hindu knot that took her feet off of the deck and left her weight totally carried by the researcher.

It made its own point more forcibly than any treatise. Whatever else, it was a reality of the here and now. There was only one discordant image that was submerged almost as soon as it appeared so that he could not be sure whether he had seen it in truth. For a split fraction of a second, as she turned, her face seemed to have altered to the majority pattern, with features suddenly coarsened and blunted. But then it was gone and Fletcher was only seeing the huge, brilliant eyes with their unmistakable signal of all systems go.

He carried her back into the room and set her down, with finicky regard for symbolism, at five minutes to twelve on a low, circular divan. It seemed to him that he had been travelling all his life towards this place and this time and this particular girl. Her image had been part of the furniture of his mind for as long as he could remember. Now he knew why the picture had made such an impact on him when he first visited Plantos. It had given an identity to something that was already present in his head. This was the last turn of the focussing dial, when the split images would weld together and make communication finally possible.

Tallou's eyes never left his face. Her hands moved slowly to the bronze clips of her notional national costume.

Commissar Hulda came out of her private cloud of unknowing in the spacious command cabin of the refurbished supership *Leviathon*. She was clipped in an acceleration couch, facing a direct viewing port that gave her a window on the square. Beside her, a voice that she recognized by its burr as Galloway's, asked if she was feeling better. First reaction was disappointment that it was not Fletcher and then relief that she was away from the mangled patrol that had rounded them up.

Free to turn her head, she checked out the oubliette and found that they had company. Two Earthmen were working at an open panel on the command console. When they looked her way, she closed her eyes, convinced that reaction was setting up double vision. They were identical and more than that, they were mint copies of the man who had grabbed for her on the high road.

With her eyes still closed, she asked Galloway for an independent judgement. 'Executive. Do you recognize the man here? Was he not one of those who brought us in?'

'I'm no surprised that it bothers you, Commissar. I reckon this must be a rare place for fertility. He's the very twin. And his buddy. And if triplets aren't enough for you, I can tell you I've seen three more, the spittin' image.'

'What happened to the car?'

'That treacherous wee bastard tried to get out at every exit; but it was no go. Then some of these zombies wheeled a piece of artillery out into the square and it was all over in five minutes.'

'Have you tried to talk to them?'

'That's no go either. Not that they seem to hold any grudge for the casualties. Either they don't lump us with the late Gimel-sin, or they just don't have any feelings either way. I'd say it was that. They're like so many androids, and that's the truth.'

Hulda said slowly, 'It must be cloning. It's a technique I've seen used once before, on one of the O.G.A. planets. Very advanced biological engineering. I don't follow the detail; but it's possible to duplicate any number of identical bodies from tissue samples. They will have used the bodies of the space crew, who were left behind when *Leviathon* was trapped here.'

'Why would they do that?'

'Maybe they wanted an expendable labour force.'—She twisted round in her straps and spoke to the nearest twin. Fletcher had said that the missing dead man had been called Geratty. There could be some residual response to a name that had meant personal identity to the original. She pitched her voice low and reinforced it with all the concentration of mental force she could bring to bear. 'Geratty; what are you doing there?'

Both men stopped working and seemed to be listening as though the voice had spoken inside their heads. She felt the strangeness of their mental responses. Wave patterns were slow and feeble. She reckoned an E.E.G. would show a curve more consistent with a corpse than a normally functioning adult male.

She tried again, 'Geratty, what has happened to you? You know this is the Fingalnan ship which you set out to find with the squadron.'

This time, there was a more positive pay off. The two men left the console and walked woodenly round to stand in front of the couches. Although there was no physical difference—both were round-faced, sandy, with the same distribution of freckles along the sides of the nose—Hulda could pick up minor differences in mental organization and the one she had judged as being the more vigorous proved the point by being the first to speak in a flat monotone.

'What are you saying?'

'This is the ship you were to destroy. Now you are helping to build it again. Why is that?'

'It is work which has to be done. We have almost finished. Soon it will be ready for count down.'

'How soon?'

'Tomorrow or the next day.'

'You will remember the Inter Galactic Organization. You were a member of that force. I am a commissar. You owe your duty to me.'

'What is duty?'

It was a good question and there was no short answer. If the sense of 'ought' had not been transferred to the new man, it would take more than a few minutes chat to put it there. Hulda settled for simple persuasion. She could not put more into his head than was there; but she could work on the basic self-regarding drives. She said, 'That is good. You have done well. Help me now and you will be rewarded. Unfasten these clips and let me see what you have done.'

The one she was talking to furrowed his brow. He had a problem. He had just enough on the orectic side to know that there was a dilemma. His twin, however, had been listening, as though it was all meant for him and had no doubts, he started on Galloway and freed his hands.

Galloway sat up and forced himself to move slowly. He unclipped the ankle bands and then was moving to Hulda when she said, 'Wait.'

She had not taken her eyes off her first subject. For her, it was a test case. If she could get him to do it, they were that much ahead in the game and enough of the original man was preserved in the clones to be subject to pressure.

There was a count of ten, with no movement in the command cabin. Somewhere below, a vibration started, as though somebody was drilling into a bulkhead. He passed his hands across his face and bent down to open the clips.

Hulda said, 'That was well done.' It was like encouraging a child.

Galloway said, 'Can you no find out what's happened to the commander?'

'Not from these men. We shall have to talk to the Plantosians. Without the car, we have nowhere to go. We shall have to work something out with them. Can you tell whether they are right in their estimate of readiness? Is the ship in fact all set to go?'

'The Commander would be the one to tell you that. It looks all right. We canna' tell what fuel they have.'

Belatedly, Hulda thought of a question that should have come up with a higher priority, 'Did they find what they were looking for?'

'Gimel-Sin brought nothin' back to the car and, as far as I could see, the Commander took nothin' with him down to the square.'

The clones had picked up the thread of an earlier programming and had lost interest. They went back to the open panel and got on with the chore of checking through its circuitry. The more outgoing member of the duo broke off every now and then to take a look at Hulda, as though she was stirring some memory chord. New-minted in an adult mould, his creators had not given him a briefing on the snares of sex, reckoning no doubt that its hazards were minimal in the restricted group he was in. Hulda's skin-tight coverall made no secret of a figure that was an apotheosis of the classical idea. A lime-green Phryne.

It bothered Geratty Multiplex and the disturbance spread to his helper. They stopped work again and Hulda picked up enough of their mental set to realize what was coming next. In a spirit of childlike enquiry, they wanted to touch her and establish what the source of the disturbance was all about.

Galloway got onto the wavelength when they packed in the electronics bit and made a deliberate pincer movement for the commissar. He said, sharply, 'Hold fast on that, Geratty,' and in the moment's grace, while their restricted computer service grappled with yet another imperative, hustled her out through the hatch.

Down was the obvious way, if they wanted to contact the main body of Plantosians; but there was another Geratty coming slowly up the companion.

Hulda had already seen him and started off towards the cone. Ignoring intermediate stations, where groups were busy on last minute maintenance, she climbed on; until they came out in the forward, gunnery control, which was the last stop before the hydroponic tank section and the automatic aerial gear. It was empty. Galloway eased down the circular plug with ten centimetres to spare from the head of Geratty Multiplex, who had followed like a Selenium dog.

Hulda sat at the communication desk to think it through. Negotiation could begin from here. Sooner or later, one of the Plantosian hierarchy would call through. In the meantime, she had another line to follow.

From somewhere, not too far distant, she was getting a strength nine signal from the wandering Fletcher. It was nice to hear from him; but having said that, there was nothing else good. Like Merlin, he was in thrall and seemed to have no immediate intention of breaking free.

Quite apart from his loss as a directing genius, there was a secondary, personal factor which she had to admit. This involvement with the lush Plantosian was no good for him. It was uncharacteristic of a mind she now knew well and was beginning to like more than any she had known. She wanted him to feel that way about herself.

Chapter Nine

Although beguiled, Dag Fletcher was not as besotted as Hulda was ready to believe. In a sequence that brought the conducted tour up to date, with a run down on present activities of the clan, he was asking questions and was recognizing that, at this level, Tallou was being evasive.

A suspicion was gathering in his head that, just as Veck had found a way to blackmail him into the mission, so Tallou had been set to work on him and soften him up for a deal.

She had made a job of it at that. When they appeared suddenly back at base, with Yarris factually present next to him at the console, his first reaction was a sense of loss, that the intimate contact had been broken and that he was separated from her.

Not by much. Her voice came from immediately behind him and he twisted round to find her. For a nonasecond, he believed he had made a mistake and the face did not belong to the familiar body. Then the features reassembled, as though his eyes were finding a proper focus.

Tallou said, 'You see, this is our last chance. We have to leave Plantos. The ship will take us to Cappodan and there we will make a new home.'

Evoked potential, associated with strong visual experience, was doing its best to knock the higher levels where judgement lurked in its hole; but years of survival by a slender margin, on the strength of giving it regular exercise, made it a slippery beast to hold down. Fletcher said, 'You are going the wrong way about it. There is provision for re-settlement in the I.G.O. code. If you send a representative with me, I can guarantee a quick hearing of your case. Transport will be arranged to take you to a suitable ethnic group, where you can integrate and survive.'

Yarris and Tallou exchanged a long look, which had no element of gratitude in it. Indeed, Yarris's expression might have been the same, if the contribution had come from a talking dog.

Tallou finally broke the silence. 'Why should we ask for what we are able to take and which is ours by right? Cappodan is a colony of Plantos. If there is an *integration,* others must change to our ways.'

There was arrogance in it, but arrogance on a scale that made it monumental. Two dozen or so of these people were ready to take on the teeming millions of an advanced, industrial planet. It was also rather pathetic. The Cappodanians were hard-headed, they would not readily welcome the survivors of a mythical home land for sentimental reasons. They would be the first to apply to the Galactic Authority to get the position clear.

Fletcher said, 'That was a very long time ago. Cappodan has developed differently. You would have to conform.'

Yarris was visibly impatient, 'It is clear that you do not understand the power we have. All that is required is that we should get there and the means to do that is ready and waiting. Your arrival has been a help, though it was not essential. It will save a little time, that is all. You will pilot *Leviathon.* Do not underestimate our knowledge of the galaxy as it is now. I will tell you; because you will not be able to misuse the information, that we have documents which will ensure that we are well-received on Cappodan. Diplomacy is not a lost art here. We have a copy of a secret undertaking, which many planets could not afford to have made public. We will use it to negotiate for a settlement. We do not require much land in the first instance. After that, we shall see who becomes the controlling group.'

A number of things became plain to Fletcher. Going right back to Veck, he saw that he had been naive every step of the way. The valuable securities bit had been a blind. This was what the Fingalnans were after and they had been prepared to ditch him and his civilian crew as soon as they got their hands on it. Scotia too had gotten wind of it. No doubt, it was some revealing run down on O.G.A. contingency agreements, with names named and information that could be dynamite if it got to I.G.O. intelligence.

Another aspect struck him. That was what Simpson's angle was. And Hulda. He stopped there. She had known about it all along. It only needed Spencer to be in the act and from first to last he had been used like an idiot child.

Spencer had hinted that there was the possibility of a charter coming up. But then, that was probably ground bait. On balance, it was likely that Spencer also had been used. Whatever his faults, the European Space chairman would not go along with that kind of chicanery.

Bitterness choked his mind. He blamed himself for being too easy. God, even here, he had been blinded by self-indulgence. Any damned girl could work on him like damp clay. Now there was only one angle. He had to get hold of that document and put it where it could do no harm. All the years of war and loss could not be wasted. Next time, O.G.A. might have the edge and Scotian predators would swarm into every gravisphere.

Both Plantosians were watching him closely and he saw that Yarris had correctly followed some of the internal argument. He looked at Tallou and had a moment's vertigo, as when Hulda had been shoving her psychokinetic probe into his head. It was Tallou, without a doubt; but the features had regressed to a point where she fitted the latter-day fresco. Her face was not entirely lacking a certain satanic beauty; but it was evil all the way. He knew for a truth, that if this clan of Plantos ever reached any other planet, the days of its hosts would be numbered. They wanted neither integration nor accommodation. They wanted to destroy.

One thing was clear, it was time somebody else was on the

receiving end of a political gambit. Fletcher said slowly, 'You put too much reliance on a treaty document. It is out of date. Governments will deny any part in it. They will say that it is a forgery. You will have to think again.'

While he was saying it, he kept every other thought out of his mind. It came out as a plain man's honest opinion, with the intention of being a help and guiding them away from future disappointment.

Yarris said, 'Not so. It will be recognized as genuine. Even without it, we shall succeed; but I will show you. You will know then that our project is well founded.'

Fletcher tried not to look interested. This was a trait he had met before. There were people who could not endure that any item in a programme should be open to criticism. While Yarris left his console and walked to another part of the horseshoe, he took a closer look at the observatory.

There was no visible door. High up, there was a clerestory of narrow apertures that appeared to be glazed in tinted translucent plastic. Above that, an octagonal dome, with alternate panels of amethyst blue and granulated silver, and, every tenth, a longer job in brilliant yellow that dropped below eye level. It was difficult to assess where the structure would fit in the main square. Not that he had ever had time to do a close survey of all the buildings. Maybe it was a penthouse addition, which was out of sight of the ground.

His eyes met Tallou's. More intelligent, or more cunning than Yarris, hers were bright with suspicion. All pretence of laying herself out to please had long gone. That was a humiliation in itself, but he let it go. Analysis could come later.

She said, 'What are you thinking?'

'I think I am in rat's alley, where the dead men lost their minds.'

'What does that mean?'

It was a small boost to self-regard that he had found an apt quote to twist. In some ways, it was like feeding a riddle to a computer. Busy trying to sort out a possible double meaning, she was sidetracked enough to hold fast on a first impulse to call up the other workers from their stations. They were, in any case, watching developments. Any aggressive move could be checked before he had gone two steps.

Two steps where though? He could not go round tapping panels for a door with four thugs and a maenad at his back. Down was through the dematerializer or whatever the apparatus was. Up then? The horseshoe computer spread was stepped by sections to a high peak in the centre. Fifteen metres from the parquet at the least count. Two metres of that pushing into the dome, with a gap that was difficult to judge between its platform top and the narrow gallery that ran below the clerestory.

Yarris was back in his midst with a flexible, black document case. There was no mistaking the cyclamen blazon on its cover. It was the vulture symbol of the O.G.A. military command, a reasonable earnest of corruption within.

Interest in the wings notched up a point. One man reached forward onto his desk and picked up a blaster which Fletcher recognized as his own. There was no chance. He was a fool to be trying. Too much depended on him. There was an eternity of time for an endless succession of decision and revision before Yarris held out the folder for him to see.

Then he was balanced on the balls of his feet, brain ice cold and calculating distances like an impersonal machine which had no part in the stress. Reaction times, refined by a thousand split second judgements in the command slot of a hurrying ship had the wallet whipped out of Yarris's hand and Tallou yanked across to tangle with the man's grabbing hands.

When Yarris threw the girl clear, it appeared to his disordered vision that Fletcher had rubbed himself out like a genie.

Onlookers, seeing more of the game, knew that he had gone aloft and were scattering to the perimeter to get a clear sight.

Fletcher shoved the case inside his coveralls to leave his

F

hands free and went up the staircase in a weaving run. One man threw a knife that sliced out a palm-sized gobbet of fabric from the slack under his left arm.

Yarris yelled something in ancient Plantosian and started up the hill. The rest waited for top dead centre and a clear target.

Fletcher knew that the plateau would set him up as an easy butt. He measured distances as he came to the penultimate riser and knew there would be no hanging about to choose the best angle when he reached the top.

There was a split second, when the scene held still like a tableau. Yarris, two steps below, going well with his teeth bared in a snarl of effort; two men, well-spaced, with right arms back behind their heads waiting to throw; the third one, standing like a duellist, with the blaster aiming for the space he was moving into; Tallou, head back, breasts taut as plump tusks, face destroyed by anger.

It must have seemed obvious that he would have to make a stop, like a statue on a plinth, to be picked off. Before they could act, he had launched himself up and out.

As his fingers touched the smooth stone of the baluster, they moved. One, confused by Yarris being where he had expected the Earthman to be, was slow to adjust and the knife took the Plantosian squarely in the throat. The other, more adaptable, shifted his aim and Fletcher felt the impact as a heavy blow in his left side. At the same time his right leg seemed to dissolve from the knee down as a nerve-stunning, multiple beam swept round.

Then he was putting out every ounce of will and strength to get himself over the top.

The knife was still with him, held mainly by the thicknesses of the document case, which it had pierced on the way to its target. It was the first time he could say that O.G.A. had done anything for him; but gratitude was tempered with distaste as he lay on his back and plucked it free. There was blood in the last centimetres of the channel and he could feel a warm sticky flow spreading inside his coverall.

Working on hands and one knee and trailing his dead leg, Fletcher covered ten metres of the narrow balcony, looking for a window he could reach without showing himself over the rim. When a yellow one showed up, he had gotten himself into a dogged rhythm and had crawled past it before it registered.

Stopped to check it out, he listened for noise from the pit. There was the sound of something heavy being dragged and he reckoned that time was running out.

He stabbed into the pane with the heavy knife expecting to be showered by glass shards. It went through as though cutting into compressed card and he found that heaving down on it made a clean cut to the base. Two more cuts and he had a panel, held at its bottom edge and almost a metre wide.

The scuff from below had stopped and there was a thud at his back. Maybe there was some doubt about who should have the honour of being first up, because there was a continuing silence as he tried to bend out his panel. Then the slightest chink of a metal object striking stone had him twisting painfully round.

A Plantosian had come up with exemplary caution and was head and neck over the rail.

Fletcher was still holding the knife and lunged upwards at full arm stretch as the man opened his mouth to shout. Following a distinguished precedent, the bright blade stood a hands breadth out behind the climber's head, when he fell back from his ladder.

Fletcher rose to his knees and threw himself at the weakened zone. He went through with the tardy thought that he could be launching himself out on a two hundred metre drop.

The pane was centimetre-thick, translucent plastic and tipped him off for a fair start on the sloping neck of the main observatory roof. Thrashing around for a hold, he was head and shoulders over the eaves, before there was a stop. There was time, on the brief journey, to know that at a basic level he did not care either way. Tallou's defection had gone deep. A fundamental proposition that people should be what they seem had taken a damaging knock. If he could be so easily deceived, there was nowhere to look for communication.

When he stopped, he was almost sorry that he had to go on. It was, as he had suspected, a penthouse development. Four metres below his hanging head there was a broad plateau of blue and red tiles. The next perimeter was a solid parapet of white stone and beyond that, in the middle distance, the cone of *Leviathon* was poking up towards the roof of the cave.

He slewed himself round and went to a full arm drop before he let go. His rubber leg buckled under him and he was half a minute gathering his breath after an awkward fall.

Walking was out and he went back to a three point shuffle over the rail. He was looking over the square from an unexpected angle. The observatory was sited on top of the end block of a crescent and was the first building from the point where the road came in at the flyover. Without any reason, he had assumed that the observatory was more central in the schema.

Over left, the roof he was on dovetailed into the living rock, with the arched opening of a narrow tunnel at the outside edge. On the right, there was a ninety degree turn to mark off the end of the block and no way to cross to the next.

There was no choice. He went along holding the rail and swinging his duff leg from the hip.

Down below, there was a lot of activity around the ship. He could pick out a number of Geratty clones, who were setting up the first stages of a gantry frame which must have been used in the reconstruction, dismantled and stowed away. They had already taken it level with the freight hatch and workers from the ship had shoved out a stabilizing grab. Maybe some last minute adjustment was required, which could only be done from outside.

A Plantosian with more time to stand and stare picked out the rooftop movement and pointed up. Every figure in the square turned and tilted his head.

At the same time, there was a scrabble from the observatory roof and two pairs of legs, one male and one with white thonged sandals, poked out ready to drop.

Dag Fletcher set his teeth and covered the last five metres with enough energy output to take him over a hundred metre sprint.

Inside the tunnel, it was easier to make progress. He could use his hands to brace himself either side. It curved to follow the shape of the cavern and he reckoned it must eventually cross above the approach road. Already, he was out of sight from the entrance, and anybody following would have to take it slow in case the quarry elected to take a little rear-guard action on his own account.

It occurred to Fletcher that, in spite of the grand design, which was their major concern, the Plantosians would be enjoying this exercise as a small emotional holiday. He was doing them a favour. Even though they had wanted to use his professional expertise, as soon as he had broken away, it had triggered off a blood lust, which was not in their own interest. It was an irrational streak in their make up. The wheel was coming full circle for them. Side by side with intellectual advance, the tide of savagery had begun to rise. This cloning technique was like in-breeding of the most restricted kind. Without the genetic interplay of normal pairing and its possibilities of selective change, the stock had become unstable. If ever they reached Cappodan, they would be as dangerous as a run-away reactor.

Ahead, there was a change in the tunnel. There was a ramp leading down and smooth handrails keyed into either side. The end was in sight, with a blank wall and the circular port of a companion leading down.

He went along sliding flat on his back and braked against the stanchion with his good leg. When he looked through the trap, he could see all of a small square chamber like a signal box with a row of stub levers mounted along the inner wall.

Opposite, the whole surface, floor to ceiling, was one-way transparent and gave a panoramic view of the city. Acoustic screening must be good. The Plantosian, who was standing looking out at the activity in the square, had seemingly not heard the movement overhead.

He was still watching, when Fletcher clumsily worked himself over the hatch and gave gravity the chance to take him down in free fall.

The gantry builders were marginally in sight from the cone. Flattened against a direct vision port, Commissar Hulda could make out the outside edge. She reported it to Galloway, who was taking a spell in an acceleration couch and he shrugged off the mists of sleep to take a look for himself.

'That's bad, Commissar, and that's the truth. It'll take the creatures a fair time to build up to here; but they have all the time they want.'

'How does it help them?'

'Well, I'd say they're anxious not to do much structural damage. Otherwise, they'd have brought up a thermic lance and cut out this wee plug. Working from outside, they can unclip heat shields and come through the skin.'

'That sounds more damaging than breaking through a hatch.'

'All this cone area comes in for heavy wear. Every ship carries replacement sections. It's designed for easy interchange. But load bearing internal members are another matter.'

'So there is nothing we can do?'

'I didna say that. Though one way or another, they'll get to us in the end. If they do nothing at all, we'll simply starve.'

On an engineering kick, she was prepared to call him uncle; but for general tactics, she had a mind of her own. 'How will they get the ship out?'

'I'd say they'll have fixed charges in that roof to blow

out a hole big enough to take her through. It's a very chancy bit of navigation. No wonder they wanted to get a hold of the commander.'

'He could do it?'

'If any man could, I'd reckon it would be him. He's about the best in the service and I've seen a few. Or *was* maybe I ought to say.'

'When they blow the hole, there'll be a pressure drop in the square.'

'Aye. The only place to be will be *inside* this ship. Anybody anywhere else has had his porridge and that's the truth.'

'Would it be possible to use any of the gear in here to breach the roof?'

Belatedly, Galloway saw where the conversation was leading him and put in a hasty *nolle prosequi*.

'Look now, Commissar, I'm an engineer. I'm no a navigator. Even if we had the ship clear, which we have not, I couldna' take her up through that hazard.'

'But the aerial gear is housed up above. If we cleared a hole, we could raise the probe, get it clear of this radio screen and send out a call to I.G.O.'

'But that means everybody outside will die. We don't know yet whether Commander Fletcher isn't still down there.'

It was a point that had not escaped her. As an I.G.O. commissar, she had made unpalatable decisions before and this one would be the worst yet. But if she knew anything at all about the way his mind worked, she knew that he would understand what she had to do. More, it was a decision that he would be prepared to make himself.

That triggered off another line of thought. What indeed did he think about her? The business with the Plantosian girl was curious. It was outside the rational; obsessive. It was not love, which was ultimately based on understanding; but something which he could not, at this stage, control. If and when, he saw his way through it, there could be danger of a profound psychological discouragement. A death of the heart.

As to that, his personal problems would be coming to a definitive end, if she carried out her plan. She shied away from closer analysis of it and watched Galloway checking out the gunnery control.

'Well?'

He was not liking it at all, but a lifetime of carrying out command decisions made elsewhere had him automatically doing his best with this one. Gunnery controls were only specialized switchgear, and this lay out was well-documented with pictographs for clarity with mixed race crews.

'Give me another minute or two. It's coming clear.'

Hulda left him to it and climbed up the wall grabs to the next compartment. Stainless steel tanks filled the space in close-packed tiers. She slid back an inspection port and saw that the one she had picked was already two-thirds full of lush green algae. They were leaving nothing to chance. There was provision for the full complement of *Leviathon* to live almost indefinitely. Wherever they made a planetfall they could sweat it out in the ship until the local population accepted their terms. And backed by the megapower of a supership they could ask for anything at all.

Up to the next stage. Now the shaping of the cone made a small tetrahedral chamber with the thick shaft of the telescopic probe as a fat central column. Local controls were collected in an instrument cluster in the roof. It looked okay. Galloway would know if it was operational.

He was another fifteen minutes checking it out and then delivered his verdict with a formality that showed he was not happy about it. The scaffold builders were working like clockwork men and had gained another fifty metres. Now they were clearly visible from the direct vision port and at the same rate of progress, the moment of decision would have to be soon.

Galloway said, 'There are four, forward-bearin', long-range destructor beams, Commissar and they can be operated as of now from this console. The aerial gear has its own local motor. There is nothin' in the way of carryin' out your suggestion.'

He could have added, 'Except general humanitarian principles,' but she read that, as a harmonic, in his tone.

Hulda gave herself a dead-line. When the scaffolding was ten metres below the viewing port, she would give the order to blow the roof. As she watched its steady, predictable climb, she appreciated the dilemma of a military command situation. Faintly, in the recesses of her mind, she was aware of a signal, which she had been trying to shut out for some time. There was no doubt about it. Fletcher was alive. He was in pain and in a mood of savage disillusion, but he was alive.

She looked at her time disk and at the gantry. Whatever it cost her personally, there was no way out of the programme she had set.

Galloway seated himself at the fire desk with its scanner turned to the roof overhead. On the hair-line grid, he marked out the minimum area that would make a viable passage and carefully lined up the tubes. It was not a long job. There was still time to fill and he sat with his hands on the firing keys, waiting for the word.

In another part of the forest, John Fergus was waiting for the word to stop and camp for a spell on the roadway.

For what seemed an indefinite length of time, it had been all go, and for his money, enough was enough. He reckoned that the crack Simpson had gotten on his head had turned him from a jokey lecher to a latter day Genghis Khan and the change was not for the better.

Even Trudy Brogan might have been prepared to cope with the old Simpson as her contribution to the public weal, rather than have them all driven by the new man.

As soon as he regained consciousness, he had sat up woozily on his swaying truck and taken charge. Being the tail end Charley, it had been some time before it penetrated to the front of the column that he was back on the strength. Finally, he had picked out a self-heating canister of Chow Mein and pitched it at the driver's back.

Up to then, Fergus had been taking it at a steady pace that gave him time to estimate the way ahead. When he stopped to see what the passenger wanted, Simpson heaved himself along, plugged himself in and spoke nastily right into his ear. 'What in the name of thunder, are you hanging about for, spaceman? Don't you understand that we have to get under cover, as soon as we can? They'll stay up there and check out the area. Just one sign of movement and they'll blast everything round here for a hundred kilometres. Double the speed.'

Complication went up by a geometrical progression. Hazards were multiplied. Maybe he was right, but he made no friends.

They reached the breach in the tunnel system with everything intact except nerves and getting the wagon train down the hole was a penultimate turn of the screw. The last twist came for Trudy Brogan when she stepped on a body in the knee-high white dust that their operations had raised.

Bramah, standing at the lock switchgear with Simpson found himself being pounded on the back by a girl who managed to mime, 'Come and look what I've found'—like a woolly mammoth gripped by polar ice.

It was a Fingalnan. Living, according to his suit gauges; but taking no interest. Fergus found another one, close by, and they propped them against the wall ready for resurrection.

Simpson jabbed impatiently towards the lock and they got on with the business of taking the trolley and its two trailers through the hatch. Ten minutes later, the gauges showed breathable air and visors were unsealed.

It was a relief to make easy communication.

Bramah asked, 'What do you make of it, Commodore? It looks as though Commander Fletcher had some trouble.'

'That's so. He's still got some, if that silvery bastard Gimel-Sin is still with him. I don't trust that one farther than I'd throw a piano by the stool. The sooner we join up with him the better. Get going, Fergus. No. Wait a bit. Get onto the rear car. I'll take a spell as motorman.'

He came as near to tipping them in the swivel-top pit as anybody would want to go. Only the sight of Fletcher's manhole cover, still beside its hole, reminded him of the hazard which had been well-documented for all squadron teams on the first visit. He shoved the trolley from full ahead into full astern as the nose was beginning to tip and caused utter chaos in the passenger area.

It took Fergus half an hour to devise a wedging system and Simpson reluctantly agreed to use the time for a meal stop.

Then they were moving on. Making good time on a clear road. They went through the first city without leaving the flyover and plunged on into the tunnel complex.

At the third, after taking driving spells all round, with one to watch and two to catnap on the loads, he agreed grudgingly to a further break of twenty minutes.

Trudy Brogan said, 'It's a wonderful city; but I don't go for that fresco. Whoever dreamed that up, has no sense of humour. But you said they were all dead, Commodore? No sign of any natives, when you last paid a visit?'

'That's so. But there have been changes I don't understand. This mural for one. I don't recall it being like this. I'd remember it. But I don't. And the roadways are cleaner. There's been something going on here. The sooner we join up with the party ahead, the better.'

They went on, Fergus driving like an android, with fatigue narrowing his mind to one over-riding issue. When and where would Simpson call a halt?

Perspective remained the same, with converging lines ahead, as though they were stationary on a moving belt. It was hypnotic and only a combined shout from all hands brought Fergus into focus with the fact of a grey wall-to-wall shutter that closed off the way ahead.

They had arrived; but unless they could shift the barrier,

they might as well have stayed for a healthy sleep anywhere along the route.

Fergus leaned on it pushing upward with flat palms. Nobody was more surprised than himself when the granulated sheet began to slip past his hands, as though he had touched off a delicate counterweight system.

He was too tired to move and was still standing with his arms up like a prophet, when the way was clear and the metropolis was spread out below their feet.

They stood and looked in simple disbelief. *Leviathon,* with a gantry doing a slow crawl up its port side, dominated the set. Close by, a tangle of wreckage was just identifiable as the remains of *Konstet's* car.

Simpson said, 'So they've bought it. Bloody marvellous. Flogged our guts out to walk into a trap. I'm surprised at Fletcher.'

His surprise took an upward twist. The man himself, smeared in blood and hopping like Long John Silver, materialized out of the stonework at the side of the flyover.

More adjusted to the unexpected, Fletcher called urgently, 'Laser. Quick.'

Military training paid off. Simpson flung it across the gap. Saw it gathered in and Fletcher hop round to fire into the gap he had left.

Over on *Leviathon,* Hulda saw the last rod go in that met her deadline. Without turning round, she said, flatly 'Now. Open the roof, now.'

Chapter Ten

Galloway, looking out from a point farther back, could not see the gantry and was ready to take a Commissar's word that it had reached a critical stage. Out beyond her, he could, however, see the beginning of the flyover and as his hands moved, he saw the flurry of activity that had broken out in the tunnel mouth.

A Burns enthusiast, he had noted that the lime-green figure in the foreground was 'backed like a salmon'. Now she cued in the next line of the ballad by spinning round and showing she was 'breasted like a swan', with a pale bell of hair swinging by centripetal urge.

Her voice, however, had no harmonic of assent in it. She said, 'What are you waiting for? Fire.'

Galloway left the desk and joined her at the window. 'Over there, Commissar. Do you no see 'em? It looks mighty like a party from the ship.'

The same appreciation had been made by the Plantosian gangers. Commands were inaudible from inside the ship, but the action was obvious enough. All hands were being rounded up to deal with the intrusion. Work stopped on the gantry, with a single spar poked up to level with the gunnery control port.

Distance was against identifying individuals. There seemed to be five, and one could be a woman. Hulda said, positively, 'It is Commander Fletcher. He will try to reach the ship.'

It was more than Galloway could find evidence for and he looked enquiringly at the girl. She had both hands on the glass and was staring as though at a crystal, with every line of her figure taut.

Maybe it was true. There was no doubt, she believed it herself.

Down below, numbers were building. Men had dropped down from the gantry and were still spilling out from below the tripod jacks. It was an all hands call. The workers in the ship itself had been pulled out.

Hulda's idea, that he would try to reach the ship, was a new one to Fletcher and came to him as soon as he had shot the Plantosian, who was on his heels down the spiral stair from the control room. It came to him fully-fledged, as the only possible way to make capital out of a terminal situation. If he could get to it, he would wreck it, in a way that would defy any power in the galaxy, to fit the pieces together.

It was an improvement on the simple plan he had formulated, when he used the stub levers to lift the curtain and found that the signal box had an outlet to the street. He was all set to drive himself on, along the tunnel, until the hounds caught up.

He leaned back on the wall and shouted to Fergus and Bramah, 'Break out any arms we have. Disconnect the trailers, Trudy. Give me a hand. Quick now.'

Using her shoulder as a support, he got himself over to the half-track and wedged himself feet astride against the front hoop.

Simpson said, *'Konstet's* gone. We should hole up and sweat it out until I.G.O. catch up.'

'Take a gun, Commodore. We're going for *Leviathon.*'

'You're out of your mind. We'll never make it. What did they use to shoot down the car?'

Answer came as a group of Fingalnan clones trundled out a squat riot gun and began a copy book drill of setting it up.

Fletcher fed in some power and the trolley began to move. Fergus jumped on, then Trudy Brogan and Bramah, hand-in-hand. Simpson stood still, then began to run and was heaved inboard as the trolley bucked out onto the flyover.

Fletcher shoved the power feed into the red quadrant for

overload and the animated tray took the curves of the clover leaf in a sliding skid, with the tracks spinning and losing adhesion. When they hit the tiled floor of the piazza, they were clocking seventy kilometres and meeting the ground one metre out of any three.

It was point blank range for the riot gun, but the speed and frenzy of approach was upsetting the clones and they were too finicky in trying for a perfect aim. By the time they had it set, Fletcher had taken a dog-leg, avoiding course-change, which nearly lost him his crew and was coming in at the defence from another angle.

The low trajectory beam tore up a spreading furrow in the tiles, that marked accurately the line he had been on. Then the lasers were clearing a swathe ahead and the tracks were biting on hummocky corpses laid out like *sastrugi*.

For a breathing second, there was stillness as they broke through into the centre. An anchorage in the eye of the wind. Then there was pandemonium, as the Plantosians whipped up the pack to close in and pin them down.

Fletcher locked the trolley to a skid stop under the gantry and fairly lifted Trudy Brogan on to the ladder leading up. She hesitated and he swiped her across the seat with the laser barrel.

Simpson and Fergus were firing back to back and with the best will in the world, the clones could make no progress. In the outer ring, the Plantosians suddenly drew together to confer. Clones were expendable and fun was fun, but the grand design could not be put in jeopardy.

Fletcher used the lull to get Bramah and Fergus up to the first stage.

Then the press in front melted to either side. A military genius had done the sum and come up with the answer of meeting fire power with fire power. The riot gun was not twenty metres distant and its operators were hidden behind a grey, oblong shield. They had all the time in the world.

Fletcher said harshly, in a tone that brooked no argument —'You next, Simpson. Up.'

Then he started after, taking the weight on his arms and one leg, with his back crawling in nervous reaction as he waited for the multiple needle beams to let out his Ka.

When Bramah and Fergus, kneeling on the first stage, leaned down to heave him up the last metre, his head was pounding with effort and a secondary factor had him swaying dizzily as he hauled himself upright against a stanchion. There was another busy finger in his mental pie. Not entirely unwelcome at that. Somewhere near at hand, Hulda was broadcasting a general welcome, compounded of affection and relief. For some reason, best known to herself, she seemed to be saying that he was home and dry.

When the vision cleared, he judged she had a point. The riot gun was a collection of trash and its operators had disappeared.

It had something to do with Hulda and he reckoned she must be inside the ship, with access to a fire control. Fair enough, but nothing could be brought to bear any nearer in. The Plantosians had grown in numbers. It was a last ditch matter for them. Standing apart, like a general on a mound, Tuchulcha was directing the siege and the female figure beside him could well be Tallou. They were racing in for the gantry with a screen of clones shoved in front.

Bramah had pushed the girl on to the next stage. Ten more metres and they would be inside the freight hatch. The whole gantry began to shake as boarders started their climb from every side.

Fletcher said again, 'Get on.' He fished inside his coveralls and thrust the document case at Fergus. 'Straight up. Give this to Commissar Hulda. Move.'

As the man was head height, he added something which was unexpected even to himself. It was the use of an old word that seemed clear and appropriate and unsentimental. It was also a kind of spell to exorcise the last traces of his preoccupation with the idea of Tallou. 'Give her my love.' It was also the issue of a note of hand that he would never have to redeem.

Single-beam, penetrating shots were too selective. He went over to a broad angle stunning beam and cleared the first wave. Knife throwers from farther back drove him in from the edge and he backed into Simpson on a similar ploy.

He fairly snarled, 'Get out of it. They need a navigator.'

Simpson hesitated. Then he saw the logic of it. Fletcher was grey with loss of blood. It was the right military decision. He started up the ladder and after four rungs, he was in sight from the hatchet men.

There was a long, rising howl of execration. A bright volley of knives blanketed the ladder in a flight pattern that could not miss. He hung on by reflex for a count of three and then went backwards in free fall, like an instant porcupine.

Fletcher stood in the centre of the platform and painfully shuffled himself round to clear each edge.

On the second circuit, there were no triers. Then he knew why. A hammer blow from below shook the structure and pitched him to his knees. They had decided to get him out of the branches by felling the tree. A second blow and the platform began to tilt.

A weight thudded down beside him and he looked stupidly at it. He was sliding towards the rim, when he recognized it for what it was. Somebody had pitched down the massive hook from the freight winch. A nice finale. Hung like a plumb bob, he would set the seal on the Plantosians' day.

He was programmed to endure and to keep trying until thought stopped. He grabbed for it with both hands and threw himself between two bending struts.

Galloway, at the controls, saw the move and keyed in every ounce of power in the system.

To a superstitious people, it would have appeared that Fletcher was plucked into the bright square of the freight hatch by the hand of his tribal god.

They were all there, standing round the coaming to see him in. Bramah, Trudy Brogan, Fergus, Galloway and Hulda. It was Hulda who held him upright, when he let go of the hook, dispensing her own particular pollen cloud which was a therapy in itself. Thanks, however, were not in season and the brilliance of welcome in her eyes dropped a lumen or two, when he said harshly, 'God almighty, don't stand about. Get this cover battened down and report to the control centre. We have to move this resurrected tank before they cut it down.'

Dag Fletcher circled slowly on the command island with an empty co-pilot's couch keeping pace. It underlined the spaciousness of *Leviathon's* control cabin. On normal establishment, there would be twenty crew manning the desks. He felt more isolated than at any time he could remember.

Galloway had four empty stations on a long power console, with Fergus on a distant wing. Bramah had the navigation spread to himself. Trudy Brogan and Hulda sat together before a bank of communications gear that would service a fair-sized city.

Ten minutes of frenetic effort had ended in this sudden hush with all hands waiting now for their moment of truth.

Fletcher had grudgingly spent a fifth of the time getting an instant suture on his side. Now, sealed up in an unfamiliar Fingalnan-type suit and held by the couch clips, his body was no problem. Except that it was tired and his head seemed a long way from his hands. He wondered, briefly, how he would stand up to the pressures of blast off, if indeed he could get *Leviathon* to move.

In the main scanner, the scene on the piazza was showing signs of rising to its own climax. The Plantosians were prepared to wreck the ship again, to winkle out the aliens. Time, after all, had been going on for a long spell on Plantos. Another year or two of reconstruction was neither here nor there. As far as he knew, they were still ignorant of the Scotian cruiser waiting outside and the fact that, either way, time had finally run out for them. He tried not to single out Tallou, knowing what he was preparing to do; but could not avoid a definite knowledge that she was in the group of Synod notables round Tuchulcha.

He had taken gunnery controls on to his own desk and he said, 'Okay. This is it. Crash blast off, Power One, on the count of five.'

At the same time, he fired the cone armament, which Galloway had re-aligned on the roof.

Inside the acoustic shell of the sealed ship, there was no sound, only a few centimetres of recoil on the massive hydraulic jacks as the power surge delivered.

Galloway saw the energy loss as a fractional drain from *Leviathon's* huge reserves. The scanner monitored it as an event out of all proportion to the simple act. Pre-laid charges intensified the blow out. Above the ship, a hectare of rock face mushroomed out and, for a nonasecond, there was a ragged oval of black sky, brilliant with stars. Then, every loose item in the square sucked past the ship in a frenzied bid for the darkside of Plantos.

Fletcher heard Hulda's intake of breath on the intercom, as the pity of it bit into her mind. After all the incredible years, the light had finally guttered out on this planet.

Maybe, later, he would have time to feel it. As of now, *Leviathon* was beginning to move. Incandescent gas was fusing the ancient pavements into running lava. Slowly, then with gathering way, the long column was jacking itself out of its gopher hole and clawing a path into the sky.

As soon as the antennae in the cone cleared the rim of screening rock, Trudy Brogan had a panoramic quadrant of the night sky on the main scanner. Without any military training at all, she knew it was up to her to pinpoint the blockading ship and hand on the reference as soon as *Leviathon* appeared above ground.

One thing was for sure, she had the edge on the Scotian

communications team, even though she was a one-woman outfit. Even a Scotian would not be looking for something he had already destroyed and there was no reason to think that another ship would launch itself like a missile from a pit.

In fact, the Scotian commander was preparing to go down to the reference he had, of *Konstet's* late position. If there were survivors, he could track them by surface craft and if not, he reckoned the area must have some significance for the quest he was on.

The course change order was rattling round the packed control cabin, like dried peas in a calabash, when his communication's executive risked personal extinction by countermanding it, in a staccato fusillade of clicks. His commander's cold mind flicked like a reptile's tongue over the new data. It was hardly credible, and he waited for the two seconds it took for confirmation, weighing who would succeed in the vacant slot on the communications desk.

When his own scanner came up with the evidence, he was no less bitter. No one rewards the bearer of bad news.

Leviathon was bad news on a terminal scale. Before her full length was clear of the ground, there was no doubt that she was a capital ship and outclassed the cruiser by much the same margin that she herself had outclassed *Konstet*. The computers had analyzed the picture and could even name the name. There were not many superships about. By some necromancy, the hulk of the craft they were seeking had been revitalized.

There was one possibility, and on it he based his move. Quick, shrewd judgement told him that the enemy might not be fully served by a trained crew. The overwhelming power might never be brought to bear. He called for every atom of urge that the cruiser could deliver and brought her round in a turn that shoved even his reptilian crew to the limit of G tolerance. Then he came down, arrow-swift, on a vector that would minimize him as a target, while he tried to get near enough to blast the supership at a range that would equalize their fire power.

It was all disappointment and disillusion, though not long lasting enough to promote a personality change. The simple fact of remaining conscious long enough to make any choice was a bonus stemming directly from the slowing responses of *Leviathon's* commander.

Fletcher was fighting an unusual personal battle on the internal front and had very little left over to counter moves from the outside. He was feeling the strain of blast off more than at any time in his career. A black curtain was pushing in on him and half his total will was committed to holding it back. Hulda had picked up the difficulty and was in there with him trying to jack up his libido with encouraging maxims.

In some ways, he could have done without her intervention. It was a distraction, knowing that she was still pitching and would have to be reckoned with as a factor in the life situation.

Conning the ship through the blow hole had taken every last ounce of concentration left over from the chore of staying towards the quick end of the quick-dead continuum. Trudy Brogan's prompt news flash of the Scotian's reference on the grid was another angle and he watched the distant silver cylinder begin its move, as though it was a fish in an aquarium and had no special meaning for him.

Hulda needled him into action. It went against the grain of her nature to be sounding off like Boadicea; but nobody else had a hot line to the inside of his head.

Fletcher got the message as his grip on the external world was beginning to go slack. In a surge of concentration, that left nothing in the bank for his own use, he keyed in the data to the range finders, locked on and shoved over the red lever that threw *Leviathon's* total armament into continuous fire. Then the curtain dropped like a black, enveloping shroud and he fell back, a lay figure, held only by his straps, as the ship lurched bodily off course.

Fail-safe gear identified the total blank on the command island and cut the pilot out of circuit. Bramah found himself faced with a command situation, as an urgent extra on the navigation spread. *Leviathon* began to spin, base over tip, in a huge, flaming fire wheel over the frozen desert of Plantos. Destructor beams going out like flailing arms turned a hundred thousand square kilometres of frozen wasteland into a cauldron of molten rock, and kicked the planet into a slow axial spin, beneath a shrouding blanket of instant cloud.

Fergus knocked out his clips and hauled himself by main force onto the island to pull off the fire bar. The ship stabilized in a dive for the boiling surface of Plantos.

Now the vectors were predictable and Bramah fired corrective thrust to head her up and out into an empty sky. The Scotian had long gone. Fifteen minutes routine work and they were buttoned down at half speed on a course that would bring them to the gravisphere of Cappodan.

Before he opened his eyes, Dag Fletcher stretched out a hand to complete the last manoeuvre he was consciously engaged on. His fingers sent in sensory clues that were way out, if they were supposed to be presenting a factual gloss on the lay-out of a fire desk.

Coming after the slow attrition of his physical persona, he reckoned this was the end of the line and dissociation was complete. No lever in his experience had carried a resilient pad of fine, silk fibre in lieu of a knob. This one took Dadaist tendencies into active surrealism by growing hands of its own, which held his by the wrist.

Vision was no immediate gain. Hulda had moved from a watching brief beside the bunk and was leaning over, to check out whether the hand bit was random, or stemming from conscious exploration of the environment.

Her pale bell of hair, swinging out between him and the light source in the cabin roof, was glowing like any nimbus or aureole. It was, on all counts, like being surprised in bed by a Pre-Raphaelite summoner to the last judgement.

Reassurance, that he still had some way to go, came as he grabbed with both hands for the spectral figure. Pain needled sharply in his right side and his hands found anchor on smoothly solid flesh.

He bent his elbows for the *experimentum crucis* and confirmed that he had pulled none other than the Bromusian Commissar Hulda into his truckle bed.

More for politics and culture than physical acrobatics, Hulda let him do it without a struggle and only disengaged herself, when the rush of activity brought its reaction and his grip went limp again. She did not, however, move out; but lay beside him, thinking it through.

The brief seconds of consciousness had been enough to give her an insight into the current Fletcher mental scenario. He was very bitter about the Plantos girl. It had knocked a very deep-seated illusion. It could well sour all his future relations with women. With herself. How far was anybody justified in interference with another's mind? But she did not want his interest on the rebound from Tallou, nor with the underlying fear that he could never completely trust his senses again.

Maybe, anyway, there was justification if one did not stand to gain? What she had in mind might well work against herself and leave him temporarily bomb proof in human contacts. A philosophic bit crossed her mind and pushed her to a decision—whoever knows what is good and does not do it, to that man, that is sin. Well, it would be good for him, however it turned out for her. She began to smooth his forehead with compelling fingers and talked quietly into his sleeping ear.

In the state he was in, he would be very suggestible. The events on Plantos had anyway been compounded of elements from a dream sequence. The editing she was doing would make it more rational and coherent.

She used an ancient technique, a secret of the few in the old culture of Bromius. He even talked to her, question and

167

answer and she saw that Tallou had filled a profile sheet that had always been present in his head. There was correlation between preference for certain types of female figure and character traits in the male observer. This choice for classical proportion, nothing excessive in breast size, leg length or buttock development, confirmed her view that he was a well-integrated type, midway on the extrovert/introvert scale and basically serious minded.

Subtly, she changed the emphasis in the recall. She put back the clock as far as Tallou was concerned. There was no change in the course of events; but she was out of the action, an unreal, shadowy figure. He would only remember the picture as he had seen it and think of her with nostalgia for an impossible ideal.

In some ways, it was true. The original Tallou of the old world of Plantos might well have been all the picture claimed.

It took a long time. When she left, he was in normal deep sleep. When he woke again, he would be all set to leap about. For herself, she selected a cabin in the admiral's suite and resolutely hypnotized herself into a sleep of her own.

Out of phase with his physician, Fletcher came fully awake in an empty cabin and broke out the clips that were holding him in his cot. This time, he felt full of sap and judged that somebody had boosted his plasma level during the night. He remembered reaching for the fire bar and had a confused sense that the ship had begun to spin out of line thereafter.

The direct vision port showed a steady star map with a paravane streaming from somewhere up forward and marking the slow lateral spin of the ship.

It was a detail that made the situation jell. Whoever was on watch was missing out on the trim. Clearly the ship was sound and, moving at this speed, under no immediate threat. All the minutiae of command crowded in. He padded round the cabin, found a shower cubicle, saw that his coveralls had been cleaned and pressed and put them on. Apart from a pins-and-needles twinge every now and then, his leg was back on circuit. He was on his way through the hatch of the control centre five minutes after opening his eyes.

Fergus looked pleased to see him. He had gotten a toe hold on the power situation, but the rest of the hardware was so much gibbering metal to him and it was beginning to wear him down like random noise.

Fletcher checked the course, stopped the lateral roll and took a positional fix. They were almost half way to Cappodan and in this empty quarter, Bramah had been justified in accepting a small, calculated risk in leaving the ship to Fergus. No doubt, the rest of the crew were short on sleep, and Hulda would be only useful as an intelligent observer.

Hulda now? She was connected with the recovery he had made. He remembered that she had been there present, beside the couch. She too would be catching up on sleep.

The log had no communications entries. So far, neither Fingalna nor Cappodan would know that a supership was on passage in the shipping lane.

Well, it could wait. Make for a little salutary panic when he appeared in their gravisphere.

He asked, 'Where is Commissar Hulda?'

'In the Admiral's suite, Commander.'

'Has she made any suggestions about course?'

'Not that I know.'

'Steady as you go. I'll be right back.'

He watched her sleeping in a nice reversal of roles. She did it very well. Totally relaxed, hair in a pale, shining fan on the head rest. Set up like an ad-man's model for wheat germ. Very vulnerable and young. But that was misleading. To get where she was, she must be very tough-minded. Steel centred under the magnolia skin.

There was no evidence, however, of metallic content, when he put a hand on the nearest bare shoulder.

Her eyes opened and she switched from a lay figure to a person, too quickly for him to draw back. A free hand came across and held his in place.

169

It was a vote of confidence which cut all corners on integration. A blank cheque to be filled out as he liked. In this instance, also, she was making no attempt to get inside his head. Respecting privacy, in an issue that was important to herself as an individual.

Dag Fletcher had a brief insight into the improbability of their meeting. Somewhere, he had heard it said that the law of chance incorporated all laws and was incomprehensible to the human mind and could only be experienced by yielding utterly to the unconscious. At that level, there was a logic and an inevitability about it. He felt that he had moved from illusion to reality. He said it aloud, 'It may sound naive to you; but I feel that the last veil of illusion has been drawn aside and you are more real than any person I have ever known.'

She was having trouble with the clips and he lent a hand to shoot them back. Then she sat up, demonstrating neatly that there was at least no physical veil in the equation.

It was a count of five before Fletcher realized that the alarm bleeps overhead were not a pounding of blood in his ears.

Fergus was pushing out an all stations call.

He said, 'Remember where we were. We can take it up from there at a later date.'

That was true too. There would be no sudden change of attitude. They were on the same side for an indefinite future. Together or apart there was communication. To know is to love.

Lacking a communications detail, Fergus had been virtually driving blind. The corvette was in direct vision not a hundred kilometres distant and still coming in like a destructive arrow, when Trudy Brogan centred it in the main scanner.

Fletcher recognized what it must have cost in nerve for its commander to get there, within point blank range of a supership showing no recognition pennants and not answering any calls. Having got this far, he would be poised ready to throw in all the fire power he had at the least unconventional move.

Now Fletcher recognized her. She was *Hawk,* Cameron's ship. That meant *Europa* would be holding off somewhere in middle distance. The squadron had come up to check out what had happened to *Konstet.*

Trudy Brogan, working at frenetic speed, had sorted out the signals and a voice came up on the general net as though the speaker was present in the control cabin. 'I.G.O. corvette *Hawk.* What ship is that? Stand by to receive a boarding party.'

Fletcher said equably, 'That's all right Jock. Any time at all. Feel free to come across.'

Even then, the corvette was taking no chances. She wheeled suddenly, dropped like a stone out of the scanner and when Trudy Brogan found her again she had halved the distance and was coming in from another quarter. She slid alongside the main hatch and grabbed on. Seconds later, six spacemen led by a huge, bulky figure, that could only be Cameron, were fanned out in the empty reception area with bulbous blasters ranging round the set.

Then *Europa,* with *Heron, Drake* and *Petrel* as outriders, was sidling into the picture.

Admiral P. J. Varley had hardly changed over the years. Iron grey hair, rat-trap mouth and a gravel voice compounded of disenchantment and the long burden of the peace-keeping role. He was, however, pleased with his inspection of *Leviathon.*

'She's sound as a bell, Fletcher. Make a first class addition to the fleet. The Fingalnans will belly-ache about it. But this will keep them in order.' He tapped the document case with its gaudy, cyclamen blazon, lying between them on the desk. 'We won't say much. Just let them know we have it. There'll be a few looking over their shoulders. Make things easier for a time. Nothing lasts for ever; but it gives us the breathing space we need, to get the initiative firmly where it should be. You've done well. Why don't you come back? There's a staff desk, if you want it. There'll be prize money in this, of course. Maybe you have in mind to retire and keep a pig.'

Fletcher reluctantly admired the opportunism of it. He had it in mind to say that he might have done better, if somebody had told him what it was all about from the beginning. But he let it ride. He said, 'Thank you, Admiral, but no. I like it where I am. On the recompense issue I would like to see the Fingalnans get something back. *Konstet* was on charter. It would make them more co-operative with European Space.'

'I'll see what I can do. A craft like this would have cost I.G.O. a packet. You'll be needing a crew. I'll send you a dozen men. Change course for Earth planet. No sense in going back to Fingalna and rubbing their noses in it. If they see *Leviathon* again, she'll have been refitted to our specification. I'll detail a corvette to take the Commissar on to Cappodan.'

It was a sting in the tail that effectively counter-balanced all the good. Though, when he got down to it, he recognized that there would have been no lotus eating for the commander of a ship the size of *Leviathon*. Even with the influx of specialists, it was a full-time chore. There was enough to do to keep his mind off the personal equation. Together or apart, there was a link that was unique. It was a great deal to know that somewhere in the Galaxy she was alive.

Spencer met him at the port. 'You're a rich man, Fletcher. Will you be wanting to leave the service?'

'I hadn't considered it.'

'Well consider it now.'

It really required no thought at all. He was essentially a working man and space was the work he knew.

'No. I don't leave unless I have to.'

'I'm glad of that. Then I can tell you, the Corporation want me to offer you a Controllership. Means less traipsing about. But maybe you'll welcome a spell ashore. It puts you in line for the highest office with the company. I think they're right. Is that settled, then?'

'If it suits you, Chairman.'

'It suits me.'

Ten days later, Fletcher realized that the junior Controller was the trouble-shooter for the outfit. He reckoned he had not known when he was well off.

For the tenth time in the morning stint, his secretary appeared, head and shoulders on the video, and asked if he would take a call from an incoming ship. With a score of nine virtually insoluble problems on the desk, he said, 'Surely. Put it through and go out and spare no expense to buy the best crystal ball on the market.'

For two seconds, the screen blanked, then Hulda was in the room with him. Carefully tuned, so that she stood at the golden section of the oblong. Dressed in the national costume of Bromius that left the heart bare to show that no guile was intended.

She said, 'I hope you will be glad to know that I got myself posted to the I.G.O. consulate on Earth planet.'

He said, 'Thank you Commissar. I do recall there is some unfinished business to take up.'

'It will have to wait five days.'

The administrator's suave robe was already loosely settled on Fletcher's shoulders. He said, 'And what are five days to what has already waited many millennia?'